PAID TO KILL

EMMY ELLIS

CHAPTER ONE

I'm bloody knackered. Could do with sleeping for a week.

Langham pressed his foot harder on the accelerator, wanting to arrive at their holiday destination quicker. He was still below the speed limit anyway but fought the need to break the rules—using his occupation as an excuse to speed

1

wasn't a good idea, even though there were no other cars on the country road or cameras to catch him. He glanced over at Oliver, his psychic aide, who dozed in the passenger seat. The poor bastard was probably knackered, too.

Langham rubbed his temple, his earlier raging headache thankfully diminishing.

Marsh Vines was where they were having their much-needed break. The string of cases they'd been working on recently had taken their toll, and Langham was bordering on burnout.

Driving out of the city's belly ten minutes ago had given him a sense of freedom. He couldn't remember the last time he'd upped sticks and buggered off somewhere without the worry of the job on his mind.

Then again, it was still on his mind, albeit hanging around in the shadows, what with the Roulette case having been so recent. But most of his paperwork was done, and Detective Fairbrother was keeping an eye on things, so there wasn't much Langham had to fret over. Nothing that couldn't wait anyway.

Langham peered over at Oliver again. The man's psychic gift had seriously evolved. He received information dumps about crimes and was able to get inside criminals' minds, reading their thoughts and knowing things about them. It freaked Langham the fuck out. Still, without him, crimes took a damn sight longer to solve.

The countryside whooshed past. Fields stretched left and right, each bordered by lines of trees, a patchwork quilt of greenery.

He checked his rearview mirror. A car was in the distance, an indistinct shape. It was going at quite a clip, and instinct kicked in, Langham estimating how fast it was going and whether he'd pull the driver over and give them what for.

Once a copper, always a copper...

He slowed, making a mental note of his own speed so he could better judge theirs if they sailed past. Another nose in the rearview. The car was much closer now. A brief memory of the Sugar Strands case floated through his mind and how Oliver had done this very thing, keeping an eye on a vehicle behind them. Except the man tailing them had been a lunatic. A killing lunatic.

"Fucking world is shot away," he mumbled, concentrating ahead for a second or two to navigate a slight bend.

He checked behind again. That car was right on his bumper, but at least it meant they weren't speeding now. Langham slowed a bit more, the speedometer needle flush to the little line that showed he was doing forty. The other car veered to the right, the driver intending to overtake, and Langham got ready to have a peek at whoever was inside. Just in case.

As the vehicle drew level with his, he stared at the two men inside. The driver, about fifty, appeared hot, his cheeks ruddy, yet he was animated, as though he was telling the passenger an exciting bit of news.

Is that Sid Mondon?

Sid was suspected of being one that provided certain services Langham had yet to prove. The murdering kind of service. The links to Sid in past cases were tenuous at best, and no matter how hard Langham had tried to haul him in for questioning, he hadn't been able to. Airtight alibis every time had seen to that.

Whoever the passenger was, he was clearly bored, staring straight at Langham. Bald head, tough as fuck to look at, a man Langham wouldn't want to meet in a dark alley without backup.

Jackson Hiscock. What the fuck are they up to out here?

Hiscock widened his eyes a little but didn't turn away. The car overtook and didn't speed off as Langham had suspected it would before he'd known who was inside. Hiscock would have told Sid to keep within the limit, and it'd be in their best interests if they bloody did. Langham would love an excuse to pull them over.

A side road appeared ahead, and Sid took it. Langham passed it, watching their progress for a second or two. He shrugged off the urge to reverse and follow them—couldn't be doing with any harassment complaints he might get if he did. He wouldn't put it past Sid to cite that he'd been minding his own business, out on a little country drive with a mate of his, and some bastard detective had stopped him with the accusation of speeding.

"Fuck it." Langham shook his head at how he just couldn't switch off no matter how hard he tried.

How *could* he switch off when what they supposedly got up to—*no supposedly about it in my mind*—came at him, slamming into his head and swirling around in there? Killers for hire, that was what they were. Paid to kill. Or at least Hiscock was. Mondon, well, he was apparently the mastermind behind the outfit, a man in charge of doling out hit jobs and sitting back while his employees did the dirty work. He lived well off it, too, going by his swanky address. And Hiscock, he earned a pretty penny an' all, as well as some woman they knew as Gail and however many others Mondon had on his payroll. At one time Langham had done a stakeout at Mondon's address, but nothing had come of it, and he'd abandoned his hunches, stifling the gut instinct that the man was behind a few unsolved murders.

Of course, Langham had looked the pair of them up to see if they had form—and had found nothing. Sid had a front for his business—a consultant, he reckoned he was, on buying and selling houses of all things. Hiscock was ex-army and a trainee in Sid's fake business, and Gail, she was his secretary.

A load of old bollocks.

One day, Langham would have those fuckers bang to rights—and he'd get a shitload of pleasure when he collared them, too.

"Too bloody right," he muttered.

The village of Marsh Vines was a few metres ahead, the landscape dotted with cottages, some of their chimneys leaning, roofs bowed from the weight of thatch. Others were more modern, the owners undoubtedly scrapping the old-fashioned for the newer, safer tiles. The road narrowed a bit,

5

and he approached at a slower speed. The street was flanked with those cottages, a house or two, and a shop that seemed out of place in such a sleepy, out-of-the-way place—too new.

A pub, the one they'd be staying in, sat next to the shop like an old man beside a young, vibrant woman. The contrast was so odd Langham was surprised planning permission had been given for the shop to be built. It ruined the quaintness of the area.

He turned right into the pub car park and drew up beside a weather-beaten wooden post that held a swinging sign proclaiming the watering hole to be The Running Hare. He left the engine idling and stared at the sign, at the image of a hare on its haunches, front paws hanging loose in front of it, teeth bared. It was a bit of an alarming picture that had a sinister air about it. The hare, sitting on the grass with countryside behind it, seemed on the lookout for someone to bite.

Langham shrugged then switched off the engine. He turned to Oliver, who was rubbing his eyes, clearly struggling to wake up.

"Have a nice kip, did you?" Langham asked.

Oliver lowered his hands to his lap. "Didn't even know I'd dozed off. Must have needed it."

"Must have. This place is giving me the creeps, by the way. Should have had a look at it online before I rang them up."

Oliver leant forward and studied the pub through the windscreen. "It would give you the creeps. A lot of people died here."

"Fuck's sake. Right, we'll book in, get settled, then maybe have a nose around. Take a walk or something. We've got two weeks of doing jack shit except resting and boozing, so we'd best make the most of it. Before we know it, we'll be back at the station, and you'll be listening to voices, I'll be chasing up leads, and we'll be knackered and wishing we were back here." Langham looked at the hare again and shuddered. "Well, wishing we were on holiday somewhere anyway. Not necessarily here."

CHAPTER TWO

It wasn't so much the drone of the car engine that was getting on Jackson Hiscock's nerves, more the drone of Sid Mondon's voice. The man had a habit of not getting to the point, going around the houses, so the saying went.

"Get on with it." Jackson rubbed his temples, his fingertips rasping over dark stubble.

9

"You just need to go and keep an eye on this bloke, that's all. Look after him for the night. Kill an intruder. Then, when I give you the all clear in the morning, you can go back to your normal little life until I need you again." Sid poked one finger between his neck and shirt collar, tugging to let air get to his pasty skin.

It wasn't any wonder he'd made that move several times during the heated journey to Marsh Vines. The fat hanging off his chin joined his body just above the hollow beneath his Adam's apple. Jowls weren't the word. Couple that with a three-piece black suit in a temperature too high, and Sid was doomed to sweat it out for the duration.

Jackson ran a hand over his hairless head. "I like the way you referred to it as a 'little life'. Funny that, because if it wasn't for my 'little life', you'd have no fucker to do some of your dirty work for you."

"Now, now." Sid gave Jackson a sideways glance. "No need to get your knickers in a twist."

"How the fuck did you know I wear knickers?" If Jackson didn't make light of things, Sid would get all serious.

Sid swerved the car down a right-hand track, slowing his speed over the bumpy surface. A dribble of sweat fell from his floppy dark hair and down his fleshy, spot-riddled temple.

"Christ, is that the place up ahead?" Jackson patted for the gun in his waistband to make sure it was there. "You expect me to be able to protect a man who lives in a house that big?"

"Uh, yes."

"With fuck knows how many entrances and windows?"

"Like I said, uh, yes."

"Jesus. You're something else, you are."

Sid nodded, speeding up. The track crossed with another main road, which he sped across without checking for other traffic, onto a smooth tarmac drive. "Yep, I am. Something fucking else. That's why you like working for me."

Jackson sighed. "You think whatever you like if it makes you feel better." He frowned. "Why didn't you let me drive here myself? Why the need to drop me off?"

"Because there's a method to what appears to be my madness, Jackson. This fella has money, and if you do your job right, more work might come from this quarter, know what I mean?"

Yeah, Jackson knew what he meant all right. Greedy bastard.

Outside the mansion—because that was what the damn place was—Sid stopped and cut the engine of his old-fashioned gold Merc. "Now then, be on your best behaviour."

Jackson got out of the car, drew his long black leather jacket tighter around him, and walked towards the mansion, giving the surroundings a quick once-over. The place stood on grounds with no trees, a home in the middle of nowhere, an instant attraction for burglars. With no fencing around the property, no gated entrance, the owner was a bloody sitting duck. Anyone could park on the track and leg it up the drive or across the grass, break a window, and climb inside, providing they had the balls to do it knowing an alarm would undoubtedly go off. He sighed at the lack of care for security and, knowing that tonight someone planned to off the owner while he slept, Jackson made a mental note to have a word and explain why perimeter fencing ought to be put up—and high iron gates. Maybe even a booth with a security guard sitting in it.

"Fucking weather. Damn heat messes with my hairstyle, know what I mean?" Sid said, coming up beside him.

Jackson gave him a hard stare. "You taking the piss?"

Sid smiled. "Yeah, baldy. You ready then?"

"Yep. A house this big, got to belong to some old bastard, hasn't it?"

Sid lifted his eyebrows. "Hmm, assuming much?"

Jackson shrugged. "Come on, let's get this over and done with so I can carry on with my little life tomorrow." He strode up the red stone steps that spanned the entire front of the building and lifted the brass knocker. He let it go, and it bounced off the backplate several times.

"Careful," Sid said. "That might look like brass but—"

"What, are you telling me that's gold?"

Sid tilted his head. "Could well be. Who knows what these snobs are prepared to spend their money on."

"And who knows what the local thieves are prepared to do, coming up here and unscrewing the knocker and flogging it."

"There is that." Sid leant forward to stare through one of the opaque glass panes on the front door. "Ay up, someone's coming." He straightened and patted his tie, then tugged the hem of his jacket. "Look smart, Jackson."

Jackson gazed down at himself and grinned.

Smart in jeans, a T-shirt, and an old leather coat? What the fuck is he on?

The door swung wide, and a thin, late- to middle-aged, greying man stood on the threshold, his hair slicked back, the movie-typical butler, a hackneyed suit to match. He stared at them through one watery eye. The other appeared as though it had been sewn shut at some point, the skin around it puckered and decorated with scars.

What the fuck happened to him?

"Yes? May I help you?" the man asked.

"Sid Mondon at your service, sir, with Jackson Hiscock. We're here to see a Mr Randall Whiteling."

"Ah, yes." The butler blinked, the skin of his manky eye twitching. "Do you have some identification, please?"

Jackson reached into his back pocket for his wallet. If Randall Whiteling thought this butler here would be able to stop someone with wicked intent from coming into the house, he had another think coming. One shove to his chest and he'd land on his fleshless arse. Jackson flashed open his wallet and produced his fake PI card. Sid showed his passport.

"That's lovely," the butler said. "Very good. If you would please follow me."

13

They entered. Jackson narrowed his eyes at Sid to silently tell him he wasn't happy with this setup. Sid usually let Jackson meet with the client before he agreed to do the job, but this time it seemed the vast amount of money had ensured he hadn't stuck to their normal agreement.

"It'll be fine," Sid mouthed.

They followed the suited spindle-figure across a foyer. Ahead, a red-carpeted central staircase was bracketed by verandas either side at the top. Several closed doors up there led to God only knew what parts of the mansion—a couple of corridors with more doors, Jackson suspected— and between each door hung portraits of austere-looking men who appeared to have corks stuck up their arses. That was all well and good if they enjoyed that kind of thing, but going by their expressions, they didn't.

Jackson returned his attention to where they were going, their footsteps ringing out on the harlequin-tiled floor. The butler stopped outside a set of double doors and rapped smartly. He pressed his ear to the wood then nodded, lifting one hand to point an oddly gnarled finger at the ceiling. Jackson glanced at Sid beside him. Sid shrugged and stared at the butler's back.

"He doesn't appear to have heard my knock, sirs," the man said. "Please wait here while I go in and see if he's ready." He pushed the door open just enough so he could slide through the gap and disappear inside.

"I swear to fucking God, Sid, if I have to spend the night playing cards with some old duffer, I'm going to bloody—"

The doors yawned open, and the butler stood to one side. "Please, do come in."

Jackson trailed Sid into the room and did a quick study. Large area, most probably a drawing room at some point in the past, now a modern lounge that stretched on for around fifty metres. Black leather sofas were dotted about, creating several somewhat private spaces should people wish to sit in huddles with like-minded friends when they came here. It reminded Jackson of a hotel reception. A cinema-sized TV hung on the wall, and he could well imagine guests congregating to watch the latest film while sipping Pimms and wincing at the lemons.

How the other half fucking live.

Sid strode to the far end towards a figure dressed in beige calf-length cargo pants and a black polo shirt. Jackson squinted to see better. The man they approached was about thirty, with long black hair and a frosting of stubble.

Sid extended a hand. The slighter man grasped it and shook.

"Sid Mondon, sir, and this here is the man for the job, Jackson Hiscock." Sid turned to wave a hand at Jackson.

"Randall Whiteling. Good of you to come." He released Sid's podgy hand and tilted his head to study Jackson.

Jackson stepped forward. "Nice to meet you, mate."

15

"It's Randall." He held out his hand, a faint smile lifting one corner of his mouth.

Their host indicated two sofas positioned around an oak coffee table laden with cupcakes on a three-tiered stand. A circle of crystal tumblers enclosed a large glass jug of some iced drink or other.

"If you'd like to take a seat, we'll get down to business," Randall said.

Sid bustled along and plonked himself on a sofa with all the finesse of a clumsy ape. Air puffed out of the furniture from his weight, and he waved, making it clear he wanted Jackson to sit on the adjacent settee next to Randall.

"So." Sid lurched forward to grab a pink-topped cupcake. "May I?"

"Help yourself," Randall said. "Would you like a cake, Hiscock?"

"Uh, no, thank you, but I wouldn't mind a drink." Jackson swallowed tightly.

"I don't stand on ceremony here," Randall said. "Pour it yourself."

Sid stuffed half a cupcake into his slack mouth. Jackson lifted the jug and poured three glasses.

"What do you think of me, Hiscock?" Randall asked.

Eh? "Not my place to say." Jackson cleared his throat. "I'm just here to make sure you don't get killed tonight. My opinion of you means fuck all."

"Jackson Hiscock!" Sid blurted, a spray of cake crumbs shooting across Jackson's vision and landing on the table. He hauled himself up so he perched on the sofa edge. "I do apologise for my employee, sir, I really do." He gave Jackson a murderous glare. "He doesn't know how to behave with folks such as yourself." Sid kicked Jackson's foot.

Randall laughed—hard. "Oh, thank the fucking Lord, I've been sent a normal babysitter. Someone who doesn't give a bloody shit who I am."

CHAPTER THREE

Nellie thought about her life up to now. When had it gone wrong? Why had it turned out this way with her childhood friend, Matilda, getting everything she'd always wanted, Nellie ending up with nothing?

Colin. It was when Colin left.

It wasn't fair, was it, to have such high hopes for the future then have things happen a completely different way. Every girl was supposed to fall in love and get married. Every girl was supposed to have babies. At least that was how she'd been brought up to expect things. Yet it hadn't worked for her—and it rankled something chronic.

She'd grown up with Colin, attending the village school and secretly hoping that one day they'd be together. She'd taken it as a given, because he'd told her when they were six that she'd be his missus. Except he'd been offered a live-in job at the big house, and his visits back to the village had become more and more infrequent. Then he'd joined the army, had gone off to fight in some war or other, and when he'd come home he'd gone straight to his old post in the house. Time had worn on, and she'd realised he didn't want to get hitched to her after all. She supposed he'd met someone else.

Of course, she was too old to meet anyone now—*and let's face it, who'd want me?*—and the time for having babies was well past. A shame, that, because she thought she'd have made a fine mother. She'd had enough practice, bringing up her brother. But there was no point in bleating on about what had gone on in previous years. She knew that, yet she still did it. Every day.

And him there, her brother, staring into space as though he watched a private film. Probably one of those filthy ones she'd found in his room. That had been such a disgusting day. He'd been at the market on one of his rare outings, ordering the weekly produce—not that they'd needed it, and it always went to waste these days. She'd been cleaning the place from top to bottom in the hopes it might make her feel better, and while in his room she'd nudged his old video recorder with the side of the vacuum cleaner, and a tape had slid out.

If she hadn't seen the label, everything would have been fine. She'd have popped the tape back in and continued in ignorant bliss.

GIRLS LOVE DONKEY COCKS—that was what had been written on it.

Well, she'd been so shocked, she'd failed to stop a sock being sucked up the vacuum hose. If the hoover hadn't protested and shouted a sharp barking sound, she'd have stared at that label forever.

She'd switched the hoover off then put the video in, turned the telly on—Lord knew why—and wondered what she'd do if the film was what the wording implied. Sitting on the end of the bed, she'd reached forward to press PLAY and waited. At first, a series of fluttering lines had come up on the screen, as though the tape had been watched over and over. Then a furry leg appeared, a donkey brayed, and a woman's face shot into view. One of those filthy women who *did it* for money.

What she'd witnessed after that would always be branded in her mind. It was something she wished she could forget. She'd even thought about visiting one of those hypnotherapist hippies on the outskirts of the village to see if they'd scrub her head clean, but those types had always frightened her. They'd been there ever since she could

21

remember, living in caravans, their dogs wandering around a scrubby yard that the police had failed to move them all from. Bloody mumbo-jumbo was what the hippies spouted, and she didn't think going to see them would do anything except lighten her bank balance anyway. So, she was stuck with the visuals.

Having them again now, she frowned and strode across the room to her brother, hands bunched into fists. She had the desire to punch the shit out of him. He always had that effect on her. She sniffed in a deep breath to curb her temper. It smelt of hops in here, of too much alcohol and not enough air freshener, but since *that day* she hadn't had the inclination to clean unless she absolutely had to. It brought back too many memories, and not just of the video either. No, memories of farther back. Ones involving her mum and dad doing similar things as that donkey woman.

Nellie felt sick.

"What are you staring at?" She poked Leonard on the shoulder.

It took a while for him to look at her. When he did, his eyes were rheumy, and he appeared as though he hadn't had much sleep lately. Perhaps he hadn't, what with the threat of them losing their livelihood. Then again, he'd always gone through life thinking everything would be fine. That something would turn up. Except nothing ever had.

That was another thing that wasn't fair.

"Nothing," he said. "I'm not thinking anything."

Sub-standard answer from a bloody sub-standard man.

He hadn't done much with his life, preferring to trail around after her from the minute he'd been born. Grabbing her leg for her to pick him up because their mother had been far too busy working alongside their dad, expecting Nellie to feed him, dress him, take him to school. Always wanting something from her, and he was still at it all these years later. Neither of them had been destined to find love, to continue the family line. It would stop with their deaths.

That was another depressing thought.

"Don't you think you ought to *do* something with yourself instead of sipping the black stuff all day long?" She poked him again, harder this time. "It can't be doing your liver any good—nor does it help our finances. And it's always me, isn't it? 'Oh, it's all right, Nellie will clean the place, Nellie will make sure everything's okay, Nellie will work it out. Nellie, Nellie, Nellie.' Well, nothing is going to be okay anymore, not with how things are going at the moment. We'll be forced to sell this place and get something smaller, but we both know that isn't an option. Not with what's out there." She jabbed her thumb towards the back of the room.

"We won't have to sell. And no one will know what's out there until we're dead." He nodded. "We'll be all right now." He blinked up at her from his usual chair, a ratty old thing their dad had sat in all of his adult life when he'd had a moment where he wasn't working.

"What, we'll be all right because of what's happening later today?" She laughed—too hard and for too long—then wiped her eyes and cheeks. "Oh, you're a funny one, Leonard, you really are. It won't help at all and you know it. Things will happen exactly as they have before, and we'll be left here not being able to do a damn thing about it."

He sighed. "I told you what to do."

She sighed back. "And I told you that isn't the solution."

"It worked before with our mum and dad."

"Don't, Leonard."

Nellie turned away to the fire, giving it the poke she wished she was giving her brother. Hot, mean, and nasty. Something that would leave a bruise and remind him of who was in charge here. Flames jumped to life out of glowing embers, and she went down on her knees to add some scrunched-up paper. It had come to them using newspapers and twigs that she scavenged from the forest that butted the end of their back garden. Coal was too expensive.

We'll die old and alone, cold, with no one realising we've even gone.

She thought of Matilda and how, if *she* died, everyone would know about it. One of her adoring family members would let themselves in through her back door and find her, stiff as a bloody board.

Nellie giggled.

"Share the joke?" Leonard smiled. "I could do with a bit of a laugh."

"No," she snapped. "It's private. Like your *donkey* video."

She'd brought that up on purpose. It always shut him up—and him being silent was what she wanted.

I'd shut him up for bloody good if I had my way. Like Mum and Dad. They'd gone on and on, and look where it got them. Out in the garden, buried under the strawberry bushes.

Nellie glanced across at Leonard and thought about what they'd done to their parents. It had solved a problem or two, and Lord knew they had problems again. But surely they were too old to do that sort of thing now, weren't they? Nellie was pushing sixty, and Leonard was an old fifty. He appeared eighty most of the time, what with his white hair and wrinkled skin. His knuckles protruded, too, like those *really* ancient people who had arthritis. She thought about the donkey video and where his hand would be while he watched it.

Shudder.

"You're a filthy, *filthy* boy, Leonard, do you know that?" She got to her feet then stood before him, hot poker in hand. "Do you need punishing?" She waved the poker. "Do you need to visit the strawberries?"

He turned fearful eyes on her—just as she'd intended—and shook his head.

"No. Please, no. Not me. Don't do that to me." His eyes filled, and his mouth quivered.

"Then don't try to tell me what to do. Don't tell me it will be all right later. Don't leave all the

25

issues to me—the worry, the stress, the...oh, everything. Get off your arse and help me out for once instead of treating me as though I'm your mother."

"But you are, you always have been."

"No." She leant forward so her face was inches from his. Held the poker up, fighting the urge to bring it down on his head and watch his skull split in two. "No, I'm not your mother. We had one, and she was too busy to care for us. I'm your sister, the person who had no choice but to bring you up. What would have happened if I'd got married, eh? What would you have done then?"

"But you didn't, you—"

"No, I didn't." *Don't hit him with it. Don't hit him...* "Because you were always around, that's why. It's all your fault. Everything is."

Leonard cried.

Nellie swivelled on one foot, threw the poker towards the rest of the companion set, then stalked across the room. She went outside to the strawberry patch and cursed the air blue, railing at her parents for being so shitty, for working all the hours God sent and leaving her with Leonard. For having no time for their kids, and when they did get a spare moment, they had that nasty sex she and Leonard had witnessed. As children they'd hidden in the double wardrobe because they'd wanted to know what the grunts were night after night.

We found out all right.

26

Matilda must have had that nasty sex in order to have children. Matilda must have worked just as hard as Nellie's parents, neglecting those children.

Anger boiled up inside her. It wasn't fair. The babies Matilda had should have been Nellie's. She wouldn't have let them spend endless days alone while she slogged to keep her business afloat. She'd have nurtured them, loved them, given them all the time in the world. Given them the childhood she'd never had.

"What do people deserve when they don't look after their kids?" Nellie said to the strawberry patch. She knelt then dug her hands into the earth. "That's right, they deserve to be dead. And what do you think I'm going to do now?" She waited for an answer. "That's right again. And it's *not* because Leonard put it into my head, it's not. It's because *I* feel it needs to be done."

CHAPTER FOUR

The pub was just as sinister to Langham inside as it had been outside. The air smelt musty, like the place hadn't had a good breeze through it in months, with the faint aroma of wood from the fire burning in a grate that belonged in medieval times. An old man sat in the far corner beside a wall covered in horse brasses, the shine of which had dulled with time, the owner or the cleaner maybe having no desire to polish them up. The old boy stared at Oliver and Langham with watery eyes, his pint of Guinness held midair, him pausing in his action of sipping.

"Should we book in somewhere else?" Langham nudged Oliver in the ribs. "The carpet—been there for sixty years, I'd say—and that bar over there looks a bit tacky, as do the tables."

"There isn't anywhere else to stay around here, you said." Oliver glanced at the old man then at Langham. "And we're here now, aren't we, so we may as well make the best of it. We only need a bed for the night after our drinking sessions."

Langham nodded. "All right."

He walked to the bar then leant on it, looking up and down for a member of staff. Their post was abandoned, and he supposed it would be if customers were few and far between. A woman of about seventy poked her head through a doorway at the other end, smiled brightly, and lifted the hatch to bustle along behind the bar to stand in front of them.

"What can I do you for?" She chuckled at her joke and placed her meaty hands on the counter, breathing as though she suffered from asthma. She was of the larger persuasion, all big boobs and round belly, her floral apron stretched across it, the material taut. Her cheeks were red and shiny, and her short hair looked in need of a good wash, as did her hands. There was dirt beneath her nails, as though she'd been gardening.

Her body hygiene and the state of the place didn't bode well.

"We've got a room." Langham handed over a piece of paper he'd printed out, a receipt from where he'd booked through a holiday agency.

She took it from him and peered down at it. "Ah, right. I'd totally forgotten about you. Good job the rooms are clean already, eh?"

That's to be determined...

She moved away to pull out a drawer under a row of beer pumps for Murphy's, Fosters, Guinness, and some ale he'd never heard of, Grampy's Bevvy.

"Here we are." She removed a key, a small notebook, a pen, and held them up, the keys dangling from one finger. "If you could just give me your autograph." That chuckle again. "On that line there, look, next to your names, then we're all squared away."

Langham signed his first. He handed the book to Oliver and took the keys from the woman. "Thank you. And breakfast is at...?" He shuddered at the thought of eating anything she cooked.

"Oh, any old time you like," she said. "Doesn't take long for me to whip something up. And it's not like we're heaving with custom, is it?" She eyed the pub, concentrating her focus on the old man for a moment, eyes narrowing. "Glad I joined that agency thing—you being here proves it works. Let's hope I get some more bookings, eh? I'm bored out of my mind half the time."

Langham smiled, at a loss for something to say. Normally, he had no trouble getting into conversations with other people—it was part of his job—but in here, with her? Nice as she seemed, he just wasn't feeling it.

Oliver slid the notebook towards her. "Thank you."

"Very welcome." She hefted her tits up with folded arms. "Will you be needing any dinner, or are you going out to Simmons' Café later?" She stared at them—hard.

Oliver's face brightened. "That would be nic—"

"We'll be going elsewhere," Langham said. "But thank you for the offer."

"Righty ho." She gave them a tight smile, trotted off to the end of the bar, then disappeared.

"It isn't just me, is it?" Langham asked quietly.

They walked away from the bar towards the stairs tucked away in the shadows to their left, ones he assumed led to the rooms.

"What, this place?" Oliver hefted his bag onto his back, holding the strap at his shoulder. "I told you. People died here." He went up first.

"Not recently, I hope." The steps curved around a corner, the walls uneven and covered in some kind of gritty plaster that had been painted magnolia. "Or in the future, for that matter."

"Why the future?" Oliver turned the corner and continued upwards.

"It's probably nothing, but I saw a couple of men earlier, while we were on the way here. It's pissed me off, that, because I keep wondering what they're doing around here."

"Got form, have they?" Oliver reached the top and waited for Langham on the landing.

"No, but they should have." Langham glanced up and down the landing, checking the numbers on the doors. "This way." He went left, towards two doors on either side and another, slimmer staircase at the end. "Hired killers. That's what I think they are anyway. Just bothered me a bit that they're where we are."

He stopped outside room number three and slid the key in the lock. He pushed the door open and held his hand out for Oliver to go in first. They'd opted to share a room to save money.

Oliver put his bag on one of the single beds. Langham dumped his on the other one, unzipped it, then took some clothes out. He glanced around for the wardrobe and, not seeing one, let out a sigh of frustration.

"Might be one of the doors over there." Oliver nodded to the right of the beds. "Old place like this, bound to be a built-in cupboard." He walked across and opened the doors. "Yep, like I said. Bathroom, too. Anyway, why would them being where we are bother you? Worried they'll kill someone and you'll be called out to assist?"

"I should be, but that's not it, and if I tell you, you'll think I'm mental."

Oliver pulled a toiletry holdall out of his bag, the loops of the cords hooked over one finger. "Well, if you don't tell me, I can't think anything, can I?"

Langham went over to the window. He looked out, down at the pub sign that was right there, the hare's eyes seeming to shift on the sign's upswing so the animal glared at him. "Fucking thing." He

33

faced Oliver. "In my line of business, right, there are times when a criminal has the urge to get you back, know what I mean? We always have to be on the lookout for shit like that. I don't know, seeing them, and the way one of them stared at me and didn't turn away—really bothered me."

Oliver closed his eyes for a second or two then opened them. "Nope, nothing to do with you, them being here. I don't want to probe further because we're not meant to be working. But there isn't anything for you to worry about."

Hating himself for it, Langham said, "I'm going to ring it in anyway. Them out here—it isn't right. There's nothing for them to go and see, nothing for them to visit."

"How do you know? Maybe they have relatives out here. Maybe—and wouldn't this just be so amazing?—they were on their way to somewhere else, like the next city. Sorry for sounding sarcastic, but I really don't want this kind of shit while we're meant to be on holiday."

"I'm sorry," Langham said. "But I can't shake the feeling that they're up to no good. If I call it in—send Fairbrother a text at least—if something goes down, he'll have probable cause to visit them and ask what they were doing around here. D'you see my point? I've been after those two for years and—"

He took his phone from his pocket, fired off a quick text, then waited for a reply.

Fairbrother returned with: OKAY, NOW FUCK OFF.

Now maybe Langham could relax.

"That's that," he said, going back to the bed. He gestured to a sign on the back of their door.

NONE OF THAT NASTY SEX IS PERMITTED IN THESE ROOMS.

"What the fuck?" he said.

"Bloody weird. See what that Simmons' place is that woman mentioned. Can't see it being much, what with the village being so small, but you never know."

"I hope it's cleaner than this place," Langham said.

Oliver went into the bathroom then came back out, face pale. "Something's up."

"Shit, didn't the channelling work? Are the dead still getting through?"

"I can still feel them. Like they're waiting. Feels like there's three of them."

"We'll go for that walk then, shall we? Might take your mind off things. Might make whoever it is trying to get hold of you go away."

"We could try, but I don't hold out much hope. They're strong—stronger than me—and I'd bet you my last quid that when I'm falling asleep, they'll sneak in."

"If you do get anything, I'll text the information in and we'll keep well out of it, all right?"

"All right."

Somehow, Langham had a feeling that Oliver knew that wouldn't be the end of it, that the pair of them wouldn't be able to ignore a new case if one came up. Fairbrother was well able to deal with things back at the station—he could bring Sergeant Villier in if she didn't mind a bit of overtime—so there was no reason for Langham and Oliver to be needed. No reason at all.

CHAPTER FIVE

Jackson stared through one of the floor-to-ceiling lounge windows at Sid's wide back. His employer strode towards his car on the driveway. The bloke had left with a gut full of cupcakes and homemade lemonade, freckles of crumbs on his tie and a smear of pink icing on his jacket lapel.

"Weird sort, your boss," Randall said—from right behind him.

Fuck me. Move back, will you? "Um, yeah. Takes a while to get used to him, but he's all right."

Sid climbed into his car then reversed at breakneck speed down the drive. Jackson thought about that copper he'd seen on the way here. If he was still around and pulled Sid over, that was Sid's problem. But what was the copper even doing out here? Had he got some tip-off or other to be on the lookout for them?

"So," Randall said. "Down to business. I know who wants me dead."

"Right." Jackson shrugged and kept his gaze ahead.

Sid made a ragged turn onto the road and disappeared from sight.

"Someone who's after your money?" Jackson asked. "A distant family member, whatever? Doesn't matter in the long run because when he arrives, I'll take him out."

"Do you know who it is?" Randall had sounded amused, like he was taking the piss. Was that how the rich were, even when facing a threat to their lives? Did they think it was just a *trifle* or however the fuck they put it, something easily fixed, nothing to worry about?

Suppose they do. And it is *nothing to worry about. He's paid good money to have this sorted. By morning it'll be as though it never happened. As though I'd never been here. Except that copper knows I have. Shit.*

"Sid knows everything," Jackson said. "I prefer not to. The less I know about them the better. He's my target, someone to be eliminated, simple as that."

"Don't you ever feel guilty?"

"Nope," Jackson sighed out. No one ever understood his reasoning, the way he saw things. How he could flick a switch in his head and just get on with assignments. "It's a job. Pays my rent."

"I see. So you don't feel emotion."

"Investing feelings in my line of work leads to mistakes. Do you feel guilty employing me to take him out?"

"No. He wants me dead."

"There you go then."

"Ah, but he hasn't done anything to you, doesn't plan on doing anything to you, not unless forced, I imagine. No reason why you should want to kill him."

"I don't *want* to kill anyone, I just do."

"Why do something you don't want to?"

He's getting on my wick. "It's the way things turned out." Jackson needed to change the subject before Randall probed too hard. Found out too much about him. About Christine and how he needed to do what he did in order to right some wrongs, to give himself a sense of being useful to someone. Making someone's life better. The fact that he wrecked other lives more often than not wasn't something he allowed himself to think about. If he had his work to keep him distracted, he didn't think about how Christine had almost killed him with what she'd done, with her words, with walking away. "Sounds to me like you're trying to put me off."

"No. On the contrary, I need this done. I'm just making sure I hired the right man for the job. Someone who might feel bad about it later isn't something I can risk. Someone who might cause me problems by spilling secrets…"

"You did your homework in finding Sid. My boss trusts me. That should be enough." Jackson turned around to face Randall, avoiding eye contact and staring at the skin just above the bloke's nose. "Listen, this is what I do. I protect people, and if it means killing, then that's just fucking tough. I don't think about whether they have a family, whether some wife or husband will be sobbing by the end of the day. Might sound heartless, but there you go. It's what I do. I don't expect anyone to get it."

Randall raised his eyebrows. "I find your career choice fascinating. You look so *dangerous*."

"I am dangerous. But there's nothing fascinating about me, mate. I do my job, get the hell out when I have the all clear, and Sid sends someone to clean up the mess and take it away. You're safe, I'm well paid, Sid's well paid. I go home. Eat, shit, shower, sleep, and the next day it starts all over again. I don't discuss who I've killed with anyone but Sid. That make you feel better?"

"Much."

"Any more questions?" Jackson stepped back. "We have stuff to discuss. I need to make you aware of what you have to do in order to stay safe in the future. I'm just taking one man out. They may send another."

"They?" Randall frowned. Two deep lines appeared between his eyebrows, and his eyes lost some of their colour.

"Figure of speech. I know as little as possible, but the bloke who wants you gone has employed someone to come here. Thought you knew that."

"Yes, so there's still a threat after tonight."

"Yeah, hence me wanting you to up your security."

"Hmm. What if we just take the main man out as well? Tonight? Solves the problem. I don't know why I didn't think of that before."

"Weren't you listening when Sid explained all this?"

"Not really," Randall said.

Jackson shook his head and stared at the ceiling. "Fuck me sideways." He dialled Sid, walking to the far end of the lounge, coat tails flapping.

"Jackson boy! Ringing so soon?" Sid bellowed. "Good job I've got the old earpiece in because there's a copper driving right behind me. Have me nicked if I had my phone to my ear, wouldn't he."

Jackson's stomach lurched. "What copper?"

"I don't know, do I. Some turd in a uniform."

"Where are you?"

"Nearly in the city, why?"

"And you weren't followed from here when you left?" *Why is a pig out here?*

"No. What's the bloody matter with you?"

"Nothing. It's all right."

"So what did you want?"

41

Jackson forced himself to forget about the police. "Listen… Randall didn't fully take in our conversation earlier. Didn't quite get what you meant when you asked if the person who wanted him removed should be removed as well."

"Ah, didn't think he did. So I'm taking it another job needs doing tonight."

"Yes."

"Consider it sorted, but Randall needs to make another payment. Same amount. Money needs to have cleared before we progress. The usual." A police siren screeched. "Buggering hell. That copper's off. Probably just late for his tea. Using the old blue lights to cheat the traffic jams, the little sod."

Thank Christ for that…

"I can't see the money transfer being a problem," Jackson said. "You said the last one cleared immediately."

"That it did, but just make sure he does it within the hour, otherwise we'll have to sort this for another night."

"I will."

"Hmm. Who shall I pick to help you out? Harry's got a drug thing to deal with, and Gail… No, she won't do."

"Dean?"

"Yeah, Dean. Righty ho." Jackson burped. "Damn lemonade. Text me when the dosh goes through. Laters."

Jackson ended the call and turned to find Randall right behind him again.

"There should be no more problems after tonight," Jackson said. "Payment needs sending as soon as possible, though."

Randall smiled tightly. "I see. Good. So, would you like a tour before I make the transaction?"

"Not really. You probably weren't listening when Sid explained the way we work either. From the plans you provided, I know where the assassin will enter, what his route through the house will be. Mind you, he won't even manage to get in. I take it you have an office?"

"Of course."

"On you go then. Money first, chat later."

CHAPTER SIX

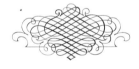

Langham held the pub door open for Oliver and waited for him to exit. Outside, he glanced up at the sign, shivered again at the sight of the hare, then surveyed the street.

"Nice little village, this," Oliver said.

"If you say so." Langham shoved his hands into his pockets.

His phone seemed to burn his palm, and he itched to get it out, have a look to see if Fairbrother had texted him. He'd switched it to silent, and not having it either buzzing or ringing every few minutes was an odd thing to get used to. And how could Oliver not sense what he did about The Running Hare? Yes, Oliver knew people had died there, but something else was going on, just that Langham couldn't put his finger on it.

"What's up with it?" Oliver asked. "Seems a nice, quiet place to me. Just what we need. Come on."

He walked off, and Langham didn't need any encouragement to follow.

They strode past the shop.

"Yep, nice and quiet." Langham observed the street out of habit, imprinting on his mind the buildings and where they stood, where alleyways were, and how many cars were parked on drives or beside the kerb of the main road.

A bike was propped against someone's high hedge, lurching haphazardly, as if it had been left there in a hurry. He gave the garden the once-over—as well as he could, given that the hedge obscured most of it. Splashes of white, blue, and a yellowy, lime-green were visible through the hedge, and Langham held his breath. A police car, it had to be. Parked on the drive.

"What's the matter?" Oliver stared over there. "Ah, fuck. Keep walking, man. None of our business, all right?"

"Nope, none of our business." But it was hard not to go and see if he could be of some help.

46

It'll just be a routine job, nothing major. Someone having a squabble or something and it got out of hand.

The thing was, Langham knew full well what the outcome of some squabbles could be. A woman slaughtered because her husband had seen red. A man stabbed because his wife had caught him out in an affair. Students, having come home from being out on the lash, getting into a fight that had turned into manslaughter. Things like that happened in villages, too.

Look at the Queer Rites case. A man strung up in a barn...

To stop images of that forming, Langham turned away from the sight of those familiar colours peeking through the hedge and continued walking. Fairbrother could come out here and deal with it if a detective was needed. Just because Langham was already here, surely they wouldn't expect him to do it.

They would and you know it.

He forced one foot in front of the other. Oliver walked with his head bent, probably waiting for Langham to say he couldn't stand it, that they had to go back and investigate. Or maybe, if something bad had happened in the house, he was fighting off the spirit who wanted to tell him all about it.

"Before you ask," Oliver said, "someone's dead in that cottage. It's one of the spirits who wanted to speak to me earlier, but I'm ignoring them. I don't want to hear it. Won't be helping them. Not this time."

"But you want to?" Langham held his breath.

"Yep, I want to. Just like you want to. But we won't."

"No, we won't." He let out the air he'd been holding in and took in the other cottages, the neat and tidy lawns. Another swinging sign caught his attention, and he narrowed his eyes to try to make it out. "Simmons' Café's there, look. Doesn't seem like much of a café to me."

"More like a restaurant or hotel. See? There's hope for us here yet." Oliver smiled at him.

They stopped beside a low wall, the top of it no higher than Langham's knees. There was a break in it, an entry to the car park, and quite a few vehicles occupied the spaces. Simmons' was another building that didn't fit in here. Modern brick, white uPVC windows and doors, a slab of decking with wooden railing around it, keeping it enclosed yet open at the same time. Small fir trees in pots positioned around the edges. Wooden tables, the slat-top kind, could easily seat six apiece.

Langham spotted a sign in the window: VACANCIES.

"Oh, for fuck's sake!" he said. "Why wasn't this on the bloody booking agency site?" He clamped his lips together in annoyance. "Would you mind if I went in and paid for a room there? Sod shelling out twice. That pub...it's filthy, and I don't like it. I don't want to sleep in a bed that might be unclean once I turn back the quilt."

Oliver shrugged. "Whatever makes you happy. And something has to." He grinned, probably to take the sting out of his words.

"Been that bad, have I?"

"Bit of a bear with a sore head."

"Sorry."

"Don't be."

Langham nodded. "Then let's go in and sort our accommodation, go to the pub and sign out, then come back here. I feel for the old dear in The Running Hare, but... I just can't bloody stay there." An image of the sign came to mind. "And it beats me why it's called that anyway. The damn creepy hare on the sign is *sitting*."

They walked across the car park and entered Simmons', and thank God, it was clean, smelt of decent food cooking, and Langham was comfortable. It was a far cry from the pub. Not a dull horseshoe in sight. Instead, a gleaming wooden reception desk was ahead, a young blonde woman sitting behind it, the walls decorated in tasteful dark-plum paint with black-and-white pictures of world landmarks.

Langham went up to the desk, and in no time they were booked in, a set of keys in his hand.

"Out of curiosity," he said to her, "why's this place called a café?"

She smiled as though she'd been asked the same question a million times. "It used to be one years ago, until my dad inherited it from his mum, Granny Matilda. We knocked it down and started all over again. We kept the name, although I keep saying that people won't realise exactly what kind of business we are now."

"No, I thought you were literally a café." Langham smiled. "But still, we've found you, and I can't tell you how bloody—pardon me—how pleased I am that we have."

"Booked in at The Running Hare, did you?" She smiled again.

Langham grimaced. "We did."

"Well, just a word of warning. She's nice enough if you stay on her good side, but if she finds out you've come here... Quite a bit of bad blood there."

"I understand. So we'll be needing to use tact then?"

"You will. If you chose to just leave without telling her, it would be less hassle. For everyone. Not that I'm telling you to do that, of course."

"No, but I understand where you're coming from. And do you cook all day, or are there specific times?"

"All day," she said, "just like it was before. We have a party in the dining room at the moment, thirty people who are nearly done, so if you want to wait"—she glanced at her watch—"say, twenty minutes, it'll be quieter in there then."

"Thanks very much." Langham pocketed the new set of keys. "We'll just nip back to the pub then."

Back out in the car park, Langham let out a huge sigh of relief.

"Want me to go in and get our things?" Oliver asked as they walked down the road. "Wouldn't want the old dear to turn nasty on you, scare you."

Langham laughed. "Cheeky bastard. Like she'd scare me. It isn't her as such, it's the building."

Oliver nodded. "Once we're back in Simmons', I'll tell you what happened in The Running Hare, if you like."

"What, about the dead people?"

"Yeah. Something to natter about over dinner, isn't it?"

If Oliver wanted to chat shit about dead people, so be it.

"So long as it isn't gruesome and puts me off my food," Langham said.

"You've seen and heard worse and still managed to eat a curry."

Langham's attention was snagged by movement behind the hedge the bike was leaning against. A uniformed officer came out to stand on the pavement, nudging the bike with his leg then scrabbling to grab it before it fell over. The poor man looked sick to his stomach, face pale.

"I'd say that's his first death," Langham said.

"It was. Some old dear."

Langham shook his head. "Broad daylight... I shouldn't be surprised, but I always am. It's like the whole world's turned to shit." He stared ahead at the pub. "And the sooner we get out of *there* the better."

Inside The Running Hare, the old man still sat in the corner nursing his Guinness. The woman was nowhere to be seen. Quickly, Langham led the way to the stairs then bolted up them, making his way to their room as though someone watched him on hidden cameras. He slid the key into the lock, going in with the idea of grabbing their bags and hoofing it back to Simmons' without being spotted.

The old woman was sitting on Oliver's bed.

Langham stared at her, his mouth dropping open, his heart rate soaring, and a knot of anger forming in his stomach. "What the f—? What are you doing in here?"

She looked up slowly, her pleasant features from before replaced with those of spite. "You're leaving me, aren't you?" She jerked her head to the side. "Going down there to *them*."

"We are, yes," Oliver said. "No offence, like."

"Lots taken." She eyed him up and down, stood and advanced towards them. "Get your bags then. Go on, pick them up. You're not welcome here anyway. Woolly bloody woofters, aren't you. Should have known when you booked. Did you think I'd have given you a double bed?"

What?

Oliver took a deep breath, straightening his shoulders. Langham fought the urge to give her a good talking to about disparaging people's sexual choices, but Oliver appeared to want to deal with this. Langham gathered some clothing and stuffed it into his bag.

"It's no wonder people don't want to stay here." Oliver disappeared into the bathroom. The sounds of him picking up his toiletries filtered through. "I mean, not only is it filthy, but *you're* filthy inside, spiteful, saying shit like that." He came back out and dumped his things in his bag, then added his clothes.

"Well I never!" She lifted one hand to cover her chest, fingers fluttering over what looked like a couple of dots of blood on her skin.

Langham peered at it, telling himself she'd maybe picked spots and they'd bled. She flattened her hand over it when she copped on to his scrutiny and glared at him with suspicion.

Oliver moved to stand by the door. Langham finished packing and tossed the keys onto the bed. They left the room and strode down the landing then the stairs, and it wasn't until they got to the bottom and in the pub that Langham chuckled.

"Don't," Oliver said, strutting to the pub door, one hand held high. "You know that shit isn't funny. It pisses me the hell off. And what was she doing in the room? Nosing about or just waiting for us like she was our mother or something? Christ." He lurched outside.

Langham caught up with him. "The car, Oliver. We need to take the car."

"Fuck it."

"Come on. Let her get on with it. She's old, she's not living on the same planet, in the same time we are. Think of it that way."

They got in and belted up. A burst of wind smacked against the windscreen, and the ominous creak of the sign swinging set Langham's teeth on edge. He shoved the key into the ignition and fired the engine.

"We're getting the hell away from here." He reversed and gazed up at that hare. "I never want to see anything that resembles a damn rabbit again." He swung the car around then glanced back up.

The old woman stared down at them from their room window, her eyes narrowed, her lips pursed.

She looked as evil as the hare.

CHAPTER SEVEN

That big bald man was in Randall's office, and Colin the butler didn't like it.

Jackson. What kind of silly name is that?

Colin had tried to stop Randall from hiring anyone to help him, but of course, things had escalated, and Randall had felt they needed protection. The problem was, Randall had no idea who he really needed protecting from.

Me.

Colin paced his room, asking himself how things had come to this. He was supposed to have sorted things out a long time ago but hadn't managed it. Besides, Randall hadn't completed his project, and Colin, when he'd gone snooping, hadn't found enough information on it to be of any use. What good was Randall's invention if it wasn't finished? Colin's boss, the man who wanted the software, had said he knew people who could take over from where Randall had got to in the programming, but Colin didn't think any of them had Randall's genius mind.

Tonight was such a pointless task.

Anything Colin had suggested hadn't gone down too well. Neither had Colin diving in to stop the last attacker from killing Randall. Colin was supposed to have stayed in his room, claiming to the police, after the deed had been done, that he hadn't heard a thing, had been dead to the world in bed. But Randall's project was near useless at that point, and Colin had gone with his instincts— to get rid of the man who'd come to kill Randall so it bought more time.

That Jackson fellow, though, he was going to prove difficult to get out of the way. Although Colin was old, he knew a thing or two about bringing a man to his knees. Knew a thing or two about killing. But despite that, he didn't think he'd be able to handle the bald man. No, he was too big, too brawny, too young, and from what Colin had gathered when Randall had told him help was on the way, this Jackson was a trained killer who had no boundaries. An assassin who wouldn't stop until he'd done what he'd been paid to do.

Colin swallowed down a pinch of fear. Things were going to go wrong again, and it was all his fault. If he'd just killed Randall a long time ago like his boss had suggested, he'd be in a hot country sunning himself on a beach by now. *And* he'd still have both his eyes. But no, he'd been adamant about letting Randall get as close to finishing his project as he could. Stopping the last killer had not just cost him half his sight but also a wedge of his pride. He'd had such a tongue-lashing from his boss that he'd wondered at the time whether he'd ever recover. Now, tonight, he would step in again, out of line, letting Jackson kill the killer. Colin risked his boss getting incredibly angry with him again, but wasn't it better that the software was closer to being ready?

He rubbed his pointer finger back and forth over his bottom lip, the nail long, the feel of it exciting. It was so sharp it could do someone a bit of damage. He loved that nail, the only one he didn't cut and, as was usual when he was alone and pondering, he raised it to the skin over his missing eye and poked. It hurt. The pain had him feeling better, more in control. The skin gave way under his touch, bowing inwards into the empty space beneath. Sometimes he thought he felt his eye in there, a resistance that stopped him prodding too deeply, but then he remembered what someone had told him once and realised that it was just his imagination. People who lost limbs swore they were still attached. His thoughts about his eye were no different.

His secret telephone vibrated, jolting him out of his musings. He dashed across the room to answer it, tripping on the rug in his haste. He lurched forward, thankfully landing on his bed, then reached under it to pull the phone out. His breath juddered out of him, and he took a moment to compose himself. If the phone enabled him to ring out, his boss would know what was going on as soon as it happened. As it didn't, Colin had suffered with nerves ever since Jackson had arrived. Waiting, waiting.

He answered. "Yes, sir?"

"What is the latest?"

"Someone is here."

"What? What do you *mean* someone is there? No one ever visits. Well, no one other than his girlfriends." Pause. "Dirty boy."

"It's someone we don't want here." Colin took a deep breath. "I rather think we should abandon tonight's affair, sir. Things could get tricky. And I know I said it before, but it would be better if you had a finished product."

"Yes, you've made your thoughts on the matter quite clear, but really, you don't need to think about it." He paused, then, "If it's just some fuck buddy of his visiting, put something in her drink that will make her ill so you can get rid of her."

"No, no, it isn't as simple as that, sir. It isn't just a casual visitor."

His boss sighed. "Explain."

Colin closed his eye and willed himself to continue, knowing he'd probably get his head bitten off for his trouble. "Randall has hired a trained assassin to deal with our guest who is due later. The gentleman—for want of a better word— is at present in Randall's office." He opened his eye.

"Oh, for God's sake."

"Indeed."

"What do you propose?"

The question startled Colin. He'd never been invited to give his opinion before, had always just taken orders or said his piece quickly and, for the most part, done as he'd been told. Except that one time.

"Oh, well," he said, stalling. He wasn't sure how to put it. He cleared his throat. "I thought you might want to call your guest off for a little while until I can deal with the gentleman."

His boss chuckled. Then laughed. Heartily. Far too heartily for Colin's liking.

"*You?* Deal with a trained assassin? After what happened before?"

"That was an accident. He got the better of me. I was in an intolerable position. As I explained, having Randall killed at that time would have been pointless for you." *But not for me. I would have been out of this mess. So why am I insistent on hanging around to make sure the software is closer to being complete? What does it matter to me if it isn't?* He wasn't sure of the answer to that. "The software was in its infancy last time. But you wouldn't listen, so I took matters into my own hands. And now you know I was right to do so. Now, Randall's so close to finishing that your technicians might be able to complete it, but what if there's some small bit of information they need—something that is vital and means the software won't work without it?"

"Has he been discussing his project with you?"

"No, he never does, but there are ways and means of finding out information, as you well know. I also decided to take other matters into my own hands. He thinks I can't get into his special room, but he's quite wrong. If you called more often, you'd know I managed to get in there last week when he was...otherwise indisposed with one of his women in that horrid sex dungeon of his."

"Sex dungeon?"

"Oh, yes." Colin warmed to the conversation, proud that he knew things his boss didn't. "There are whips and chains, all manner of things that would make the hairs on the back of your neck stand up."

His boss breathed heavily.

"So," Colin went on, "as I was saying, I went into the room where he keeps the software. There was a pad on the desk with a list written down. It was in code, and all but one of the points he'd made had been ticked off."

"That doesn't mean it's a list to do with the project."

"Yes, it does. It was Morse code. You forget I can read that."

"So it definitely isn't finished."

"No. I don't believe we even need your guest to come here. I'll deal with this assassin, then with Randall. Maybe the software is at the point where your people can figure out the last bit." *And if they can't... I need to get away from here. Start my new life.*

His boss spluttered.

Colin continued, "Like you said, I could put something in their drinks."

"I'm possibly being a fool here, but very well. How long will you need?"

"A couple of hours."

"They're yours. When I call back, I expect both jobs to have been done. Then I'll send my men to collect the software and the bodies. If you don't answer the phone, I'll take it you've been overpowered and our original plan will go ahead."

"Thank you, sir."

"Don't make me regret this, Colin."

"Oh, you won't."

The call was cut from the other end, leaving Colin a little bereft that he hadn't been wished luck or to break a leg. Then again, the latter comment might well have given him a sense of foreboding, and he couldn't have that.

No, because at the moment, he puffed his chest out, full of pride and purpose. He was useful again, like he'd been in the war. And that was something he'd wanted for longer than he cared to admit.

His good eye prickled then filled, and he dashed the dampness away. He wasn't crying. He didn't cry. His eye was just watering, that was all.

He stowed the phone back under the bed and left his room. Quietly, he walked towards Randall's office. Pressed his ear to the door.

"It's rather an expensive racket your boss is running," Randall said.

"It has to be. We're risk-takers, people who do what the majority wouldn't. We have the threat of being caught to deal with."

"Yes, I understand the cost, and I certainly don't mind paying it, but what I was implying was, why don't you go out on your own? Why don't you take the full price instead of a cut?"

The bald man coughed. "Because this way I don't have to dump bodies or do anything much except kill. If I had to do what Sid does and make the plans beforehand, set up the meetings with clients, do the job and then the clean-up, well, it's quite a bit of work. I might not be as sharp as I should be by the time the kill comes around."

"I see. So starting over somewhere else with your kind of job isn't something you'd contemplate then?"

Why is Randall asking such a question? Or is he just making polite conversation?

Suspicion sent Colin antsy, and he shifted from foot to foot. The floor creaked. He held his breath. The conversation in the room had stopped. Thinking it better that he disappear rather than risk getting caught listening, he stepped back, away from the noisy floorboard, and went to his room.

He wanted to sit and think about what he'd heard. Something told him there was more to that conversation. Something he ought to know about.

CHAPTER EIGHT

Jackson left Randall's office and headed to the foyer to send Sid the agreed text about the money transfer. He received a reply almost immediately, saying things were on the move. He slid his phone into his back pocket.

He stared at a chandelier, the dangling, tear-shaped glass droplets catching the fading sunlight streaming through a row of large windows above the front door. The foyer had to be about half the size of Jackson's penthouse apartment. He wondered what Randall's family had done over the years to enable them to afford such a luxurious place—or whether the mansion hadn't been handed down to him from a long line of ancestors at all. Maybe he'd just bought it. The estimated cost of the place, and of running it, was enough to boggle Jackson's mind. And he'd thought *he* was rich. What the hell did Randall do for a living, if anything? Jackson suddenly found himself wishing that he'd asked for more background.

He thought about why he did this job. Why he had to keep his mind busy.

Jackson had been away with the army, had come home on unexpected leave to find Christine enjoying someone else's attention. Jackson had stood shocked in the bedroom doorway. He'd never forget that smug smile of hers, the exaggerated groan as she'd stared into Jackson's eyes. Would never forget the young bloke in his bed, lifting his head to find Jackson there and not even flinching.

Don't think about it.

Seemed it was too bloody late. The floodgates had opened, and everything from that day came roaring back on a wave of gut-twisting pain. Their languid rise from the bed, the pair of them casually dressing as though Jackson didn't exist. The long, slow kiss in front of the bedroom window, the sunlight rendering them silhouettes. Light touches using hands that had clearly already been to those places several times before. Jackson rooted, unable to move, the big, tough army man who couldn't speak a fucking word. His throat had tightened, his eyes had stung, and he'd watched it all, blinking, blinking, and wishing he was still on duty in the dirt, rifle raised, him ready to shoot the first motherfucker who came out of hiding. Him stupidly thinking Christine had waited for him at home, as faithful as her letters had said she was.

Hadn't fucking happened like that, though, had it?

After dressing, Christine's lover had swept past, giving a taunting finger-waggle of a wave, leaving their flat with an uncharitable slam of the front door. That noise had woken Jackson up, had forced him to step into the bedroom and gather his belongings. He'd stuffed them into a suitcase without a word, without looking at Christine, who'd flopped back onto the bed, body on show, a final taunt as to what was no longer his.

The memory of leaving that flat had been a blur—still was. He'd found himself at his mother's and holed up in his childhood bedroom for the week, then had returned to duty a changed man. He no longer felt guilty if he killed someone, because every time he did, he was killing Christine and what she'd done. He no longer had sleepless nights wondering how long the affair had been going on, why he hadn't been enough to wait for.

No longer gave a shit about anything much.

Randall came out into the foyer, and Jackson jumped.

He needed to remain vigilant. He hadn't heard the man coming, and that wasn't good. If he did that tonight, lost concentration, he'd be right in the shit.

CHAPTER NINE

Langham's dinner was going down a treat. Steak and chips with peas and half a grilled tomato on the side. "Did you notice anything about that woman?"

"Which one, the waitress?" Oliver drew his eyebrows together. "Nope. She looked like any other young girl to me. Why?" He speared a chip with his fork then stuck it in his mouth.

"Not her. She was fine. I meant the old woman in The Running Hare."

Oliver swallowed. "I sensed something about her the minute she appeared from that doorway in the bar—you know, the first time we saw her."

Langham cut into his steak. Pink juices seeped out onto his plate. "She was angry, possibly hurt that we were leaving. What did you sense about her?"

"I got the idea she'd been up to something. Like she'd been doing something before we'd turned up. Her face was red, if you remember, and it looked like her hair was greasy, but thinking about it now, it could just have been wet. When we went back to get our bags, her hair was dry, clean."

"Hmm. So what are you suggesting?"

"I don't know. She could have been washing her hair in the kitchen when we got there—assuming that was a kitchen she'd come out of. Maybe she was flustered at seeing us, hence the red face. And she said she'd forgotten we were coming, remember? Old people get like that. Forgetful. But she definitely dried her hair while we were gone."

Langham nodded. Remembered her chest. The spots.

Oliver went on, "So why did you want to know whether I noticed anything about her?"

"She had dots of blood on her chest, and it's bothered me ever since I saw them. I didn't see them when we got the keys off her, but in our room, she lifted her hand to her neck, and it drew my attention. Coupled with what you've just said, about her seeming to have been up to something..." He shook his head. "A copper's crap. Ignore me."

Oliver gave his dinner his full attention. Langham ate the last piece of his steak. Oliver stared through the restaurant window, down the street in the direction of the cottage with the high hedge. Langham resisted turning around to see what was going on. He'd uphold his side of the bargain and pretend nothing untoward had happened there. And if Oliver hadn't told him someone was dead, he wouldn't know exactly what had occurred anyway, just that a policeman had visited the premises.

"The old dear in that cottage," Oliver said. "She's pressing me. It hurts to deny her."

Shit.

"Hurting how?" Langham asked.

"Making me feel bad. She needs my help—our help—and knows I'm preventing her from speaking to me. She doesn't understand why, I can feel it." He jerked his head at the window. "There's a copper coming over here. Fairbrother might have told him you're in the village."

"Oh, for fuck's sake..." Although he'd wanted to help, had felt he needed to, now that an officer might well be coming over here to ask him, it bugged him. It was different, wasn't it, offering help as opposed to being *asked* or told to. "He might not be coming over here for that at all. Fairbrother thinks we're staying at that bloody pub, and I haven't told him otherwise. Haven't looked at my phone since I texted him. So eat your dinner, ignore the spirit."

Oliver continued to stare down the road.

"And," Langham said, "giving her cottage your attention isn't going to help, is it? A tether, that's what you're making it, something that links you to her. Stop looking, stop giving her something to grab on to."

"But she's found me anyway. Makes no difference *what* I look at now. I just need to concentrate on keeping her out."

Langham let air out slowly. "Fair enough." He ate some chips then cut his tomato up. The seeds oozed and settled on his plate like snot. His stomach churned, and he pushed his plate away, no longer hungry.

A scream rent the air. Langham jumped up and took stock of the dining room. The large group of diners had left. A married couple were eating on the opposite side, darting their heads back and forth between him and the dining room door. Langham glanced at Oliver apologetically and rushed towards where the scream had come from—somewhere out in reception. He burst through the doorway, met with the scene of the blonde receptionist crumpled in a police officer's arms, her legs bent at the knees as though they'd given way, the officer clearly struggling to hold her up.

"Here, let me help." Langham strode across the foyer and took the woman into his arms. "I'm a detective, by the way," he said to the officer. "I'll show you my ID in a second. Let's just get this lady settled." To her, he said, "Is there a back room, love? Somewhere I can take you?"

She nodded, her cheek rasping on his shirt. "The d-door behind the d-desk."

He jerked his head at the officer and led the way to the room. It held a sofa against the back wall, a coffee table in front of it, a few magazines scattered on top. Langham lowered her to the sofa and sat beside her, keeping one arm around her back. Whatever had her screaming had shocked the life out of her. She'd gone pale and looked like she could barely think straight.

"What's happened?" Langham stared up at the officer while fishing in his pocket for his ID. He showed it, then, when the man seemed satisfied, tucked it away. "Is this to do with what's going on over the road?"

"The young lady here is related to the deceased at the address I've just come from. It's her gran, sir."

Oh shit. "Right." Langham gave the blonde a reassuring squeeze and checked her face for signs of severe distress. "Is your dad about, love? Or someone else we can get hold of to sit with you?"

"He's at home," she whispered. "Upstairs on the top floor. We live up there. Through that other door."

"Okay." Langham glanced up at the officer again. "Would you sit with her while I go and see him?"

"Yes, sir."

Langham exited the room via a second door that led directly to a set of stairs, then another set as he guessed he was going to the very top, perhaps to what would normally be the attic space. He knocked on a door and waited for it to open.

A man of about fifty stood there, salt-and-pepper hair brushed back from his face, messy, as though he'd run his hands through it recently. He frowned. "Yes? How did you get up here?"

Langham showed him his ID. "You'll need to come downstairs, sir." He was tempted to explain, but it wasn't his case. "There's an officer who needs to speak to you."

He rolled his eyes. "Not another complaint, surely. I come up here for a bit of shut-eye, and look what happens. Her down the road starts."

"Her down the road?" Langham stepped back.

The man made his way downstairs. "Yes, the woman at The Running Hare," he said over his shoulder. "Always making things up, phoning the police with fake incidents."

Langham followed him down.

"I can tell you I've been up here asleep," the man said. "I've not done anything to her. I haven't even spoken to her for weeks. Best to avoid her, I think, otherwise it gives her ammunition."

"That's sensible," Langham said. "Could you wait there a minute? Don't go through into that room just yet."

The father paused at the bottom of the stairs. He stared at Langham and frowned. "This isn't about her, is it?"

Langham joined him. "No, sir, I'm afraid it isn't. Just wait there a second, all right?" He went into the room, closed the door, then motioned for the officer to come over. "Her father's just out there. I'll leave you to it. I would stay to help, but I'm on holiday. I'm staying here, should you need me for advice or whatnot, but anything else, you're on your own."

"Thank you, sir."

Langham would normally have checked with the woman to see if she was all right, but he steeled himself against going over to her and strode out instead, leaving her grief behind. He went back into the dining room and sat.

"What happened?" Oliver was still eyeing the cottage over the road.

"The old lady who got killed. She's the receptionist's gran. I made sure she was okay then went up to get her dad. Whether the dead woman is his or his wife's mother, I have no idea. I didn't hang around to find out. Left it to the officer who'd broken the news to the receptionist. She hasn't taken it well, but then who would?"

Oliver didn't turn from the window. "We're going to get brought into this, you know that, don't you?"

"We're bloody not." Langham took a sip of water. It eased his parched throat from the adrenaline rush. "I'm telling you, they can get on with it."

"I suspect we'll have no choice." Oliver sounded distant.

"What do you mean, we'll have no choice? Of course we've got a bloody choice. We didn't see anything, we know nothing. First we knew of it was seeing the patrol car on the drive. We didn't hear a thing, see a thing."

"What about if someone else butts in and we're forced to help?"

"Forced? What, d'you think Fairbrother or whoever is going to turn up here will *make* me go back to work? Really?"

Why did Oliver appear so vacant, so out of sorts, so riveted to the cottage?

"Don't be angry with me," Oliver said.

"Angry about what?"

Oliver continued his study of the cottage. Langham's heart rate kicked up again, another surge of adrenaline streaking through him, and on top of what had already flooded his system, he was a bit off kilter.

Langham frowned. "Will you just spit it out? What's the matter?"

Oliver finally pulled his gaze from outside and looked at Langham. "I let her in. I let the dead lady speak to me."

"Shit," Langham said. "I thought it might be too much for you. Keeping her out, I mean. Are you all right?"

"Not too bad. I've been worse. But when I said we were going to get dragged into it, believe me, we are."

"What did she say to you? Tell me from the beginning." Langham glanced at Oliver's glass. It was still full of water. "Do you need a drink? As in, a proper drink?"

"In a minute. Let me get this out first, so I don't forget. It's important."

Langham drummed the fingers of one hand on his thigh. *He* needed a proper drink, but he was buggered if he'd get up. And calling a waitress when the hotel staff were in mourning—no, they could go into the bar in a bit. And going back to The Running Hare for a swift pint wasn't something he'd do no matter how much he needed some alcohol.

Oliver released a long breath. "She burst in, flooded me with her spirit. I felt sick, like she'd infected me with something. She said who she was and babbled at me, her words tumbling out so they didn't make sense. I asked her—in my head, what with that couple sitting over there—to calm down or to show me pictures instead. I could hear her breathing as she thought about how to do it. I mean, it's not something I imagine they just know how to do, transferring images like that. But she managed it. The problem was, they were worse than her words. They all meshed together and made this thing like a vortex, as though all the pictures she was showing me were being sucked down a plughole."

He rubbed his hands up and down his face, and Langham wondered if Oliver was seeing it all again.

"It fucking hurt my head. Then she seemed to get the hang of it, to get herself calm, and she spoke again, and this time it was slower. She said she'd been knitting, watching the twenty-four-hour news about someone who'd broken into a house, would you believe. Someone banged on her back door, she said, and she jumped—the story on the news had got her jittery. Anyway, she went to see who it was, thinking it would be a family member, because all of her family knew not to knock on her front door."

"So she wasn't afraid of who would be at the door." Langham grimaced. "Whoever killed her knew that her family always went around the back. Someone who lives here then, or knows the family. That narrows it down."

"I thought the same, so I asked her if it was someone she knew. She said she knew her all right."

"Her?" *Jesus wept.*

"Yes, her."

"Did she tell you who it was?"

"Not yet."

"So what happened next?"

"She let her in, thinking they'd have another row, that the woman would say her piece then go away again like she'd done before. But she didn't. She said she had some people coming to visit—the killer did—and that before the old woman could get her hands on them, she was going to sort her out."

Langham swallowed a slew of bile that had zipped up into his throat. This didn't sound good. "Ask her now. I don't want to know how she got killed, I just want to know who did it."

Oliver closed his eyes and mumbled a few words, then said louder, "She's whispering. I can't make out what she's saying. Sounds like, 'Tell him. Tell him what I said first.' Right. So the killer pushed her down onto her sofa then knelt on her chest, pinning her there. She was angry, probably how she had the strength to do that, and bent over, putting her hands around her throat. She squeezed, and the woman, the one being killed, coughed. A spray of blood came out—like a fine mist—and went on the killer and... Shit, it's her from The Running Hare, isn't it?" He stared at Langham, eyes wide as realisation hit him.

"That's what I thought." Langham shook his head. "And afterwards she went home, scrubbed her face—which is why it was so red—and washed her hair. Except she didn't wash her chest properly. I can see it all now, how she would have rushed because she knew we were coming. She hadn't 'totally forgotten' our arrival at all."

"She killed because of us, because we were coming to stay." Oliver blinked several times.

"No, not because of us specifically. It could have been anyone booking a room there. She'd got herself so pissed off with this place getting all the guests it tipped her over the edge. And when she was in our room, and we came back, she knew we were leaving. She'd probably watched us come here. And now she'll be angry, or maybe even disillusioned, about how she killed and we left her anyway. And think about it, she must be deranged. How would killing the gran stop people staying here? Wouldn't she have to kill the receptionist or her father? Her mother, if she has one around? And *this*," Langham said, reaching into his pocket, "I *have* to call in."

He switched his ringer and vibrate alerts back on, then selected Fairbrother's number from his contact list.

Fairbrother took a while to answer. "What are you doing ringing me?"

"I know I said I wouldn't but—"

"And if it's about Mondon and Hiscock, Mondon's at home, but I don't have a location for Hiscock yet. I can handle them. Have your holiday."

"It isn't about them."

"Oh. Right. What *is* it about?"

"Has our division had a call about a murder in Marsh Vines?"

"Oh, you're kidding me? Does crime follow you or what?"

"Seems that way."

"I haven't been called out to anything, but I can check whether someone else has."

"You'll need to. I know who the killer is and why she did it."

Fairbrother sighed. "Okay, give it to me. *Then* go back to your holiday."

"We'll be leaving in the morning," Langham said. "If you don't mind, that is."

He sat next to Oliver in the bar, in one corner beside a jukebox that stood silent. He was grateful it wasn't belting out any noise—he couldn't be doing with that at the moment. He had a pint of Guinness in his hand, which reminded him of the man in The Running Hare. Had the old duffer known what the pub owner was going to do? Was he her husband? Was that why he'd stared at them the way he had, as though they had no right being there, arriving just a little bit early while she'd been murdering?

Oliver swallowed a mouthful of lager. "No, I don't mind. Where will we go?"

"Home."

"Oh."

"To pick up our passports, make a last-minute booking online for abroad, then we're fucking off. What do you fancy? My treat."

"Anywhere other than England. Somewhere we can't be called back from easily. Unless one of our family members is in an accident or something." Oliver paused, seeming thoughtful. "But since we went and visited my mum and she made it even clearer she wants nothing to do with me, I might not even come back from abroad if she was ill."

Langham put his Guinness down. "I don't have anyone. Haven't had for years. Had the same problem as you. Family turfed me out, you know the score. So if we got a call when we were abroad saying my mother or father had died, I wouldn't be rushing back either."

CHAPTER TEN

Nellie was still in the gay boys' bedroom, staring out of the window. She'd been rooted to the spot and had no inclination to move ever since the men had left. But she'd have to soon. She had plans to make, other people to get rid of. Except things had gone awry, and she had to work out what to do next. Once she'd killed Matilda—

and it had been easier than she'd thought—she'd left via the back, the same way she'd gone in. She hadn't crossed the street in plain view going there or back, instead preferring to walk around the rear of all the houses so there was less chance of her being seen. Everyone who lived at this end of the street was at work during the day, only Matilda being at home. Nellie's entrance and exit had been more or less safe.

But she hadn't expected one of Matilda's grandchildren to turn up over the road while Nellie had been booking the gays in. When the men had left and she'd looked out of the window and had seen the bike, she'd known her plans had gone wrong. No one usually visited Matilda until after eight at night, to check and ensure she was okay. So why had that grandson arrived? Was Matilda even dead? Had she managed to come back to life and phone for help?

I'll be caught.

Nellie's stomach churned. The last thing she needed was to spend the rest of her life in prison. That would be typical, too—nothing had gone the way it should have for her, so why would now be any different?

She watched as another police car turned up. Two men got out, one in uniform, the other in a suit. The suited one went into Matilda's house then came out again and headed towards Nellie's pub.

Matilda's told them it was me. She's alive.

A streak of fear went through her so quickly and violently she staggered a bit and gripped the windowsill. The man turned and called out to the other officer, who followed him. Knowing what she had to do, Nellie dashed downstairs as fast as she was able and went through the pub lounge.

"What's the hurry?" Leonard leant forward to place his pint glass on the table.

"Shut your bloody face," she said. "Be quiet—and I *mean* quiet. Silent."

She strode to the front door, locked it, then rushed to close all the curtains. Once done, she went out the back to secure the door there. She stared at the strawberry patch through the glass.

"This is all your fault," she said, narrowing her eyes and homing in on a shrivelled piece of fruit sitting on top of a withered, yellowing leaf. "You didn't bring us up properly, and now look what's occurred. I have to do things a person shouldn't be doing, and it's sinning, me doing them. Sinning."

She snapped the blind closed and returned to the lounge, out of breath, her heart hammering far too madly. Deep breath taken, she collected a roll of duct tape from the drawer beneath the bar and popped it into the pocket on the front of her apron. One of the twigs crackled in the grate, and she took it as a sign that she needed to get a move on. She may not have done what she wanted with her life, but it was clear she was being directed. Small signs like that twig popping had guided her all along, she just hadn't acknowledged their importance until now.

Patting her apron pocket, she went around the other side of the bar and walked to the fire. Picked the poker up. It was heavy, a nice, nerve-steadying kind of weight, and she prodded the embers, hoping they'd heat the metal to a satisfying degree. She rested the poker on the grate, the tip still in the orange glow, and went to sit beside Leonard.

"Remember what I said." She nudged him with her elbow. "Be quiet."

Someone pushed at the front door. Nellie held her breath, feeling as if she could be seen even though she'd closed the curtains. Her blood ran cold through fear of being stopped before she could start what she needed to finish.

Go away. Just for a little while.

A loud rap on the door almost had her shrieking with anger, but she held it in. She didn't dare look at Leonard, who, in her peripheral vision, stared at her, whittling his shirt collar with his spindly little fingers. How she hated those fingers, those knuckles. They were twinned in her mind with donkeys and women of the night. Leonard was no better than those gays, what with him loving to watch that nasty sex business.

The door was banged again.

Half an hour, that's all I need, then you can come in.

Nellie sat in silence beside Leonard for five minutes, then got up to push one of the curtains aside and peer out. The policemen had gone, and she peered over at Matilda's to see what was what there. Another police car had arrived. Crime scene tape had been attached to the fence. It flapped in the breeze where it hung from the hedge. Happy the police were busy, she let the curtain fall back into place and bustled over to the fire.

"You know, Leonard," she said, picking up the poker and making sure it was firm in her grip, "I did what you suggested earlier, and it went wrong. I knew I should have ignored you, but I went out to speak to Mum and Dad and got myself all annoyed. I visited Matilda, thinking that if she was gone I could then sort the rest of her family out and we'd get all the business again—and it would have worked, too, if it wasn't for that grandson of hers."

"What do you mean?"

She moved to stand in front of him, flexing her fingers around the poker handle. "What do I mean? I sent her off to the Pearly Gates, didn't I, and her grandson came to see her early. The police are there. Matilda can't have died—she must have telephoned for help. Told them what I'd done."

"And what did you do?"

"What? Are you thick? I thought I'd *killed* her, Leonard. Strangled her. Except I obviously didn't strangle her for long enough. Those people who knocked on the door? Police, that's who they were." She leant forward for emphasis. "Coming to get us. Get me, then get you when they discover the strawberry patch."

Leonard lifted his hands to cover his ears. "Stop it, Nellie. I don't want to hear things like that. What will we do?"

"I don't know what *we'll* do, but I know what *I'm* going to do. Hold this for me."

She thrust the poker towards him. He took it, and she removed the duct tape from her pocket. Pulled a strip free then bit a piece off. Threw the roll to the floor. Leonard stared at her, clearly puzzled as to what she was doing, but his expression held no fear. She slapped the tape across his mouth. Snatched the poker. She raised it then brought it crashing down on his white-haired head with massive force. A thud and a crack sounded simultaneously, followed by a wet *thwack*. Leonard screamed, the noise muffled, and she hit him again and again.

She couldn't have him telling them what she'd done to their parents and Matilda. To anyone who had pissed her off over the years. Guests or passersby who had popped in for directions. She'd taken all her anger out on them. Anger over Matilda living the life Nellie had wanted. Anger that life was so sodding unfair.

Covered in blood spatter, she dropped the poker to the floor and made her way upstairs. In her bathroom, she unscrewed the cap of a tablet bottle and stuffed the contents in her mouth. Swallowed them down with water from the tap, annoyed that they'd decided to create what felt like a ball in her windpipe. At her bedside cabinet, she opened the drawer and took out a bottle of gin, staring down at it and anticipating the taste.

She wandered down the landing until she reached her parents' old room. Opened the door. Stood and stared. Everything was the same as it had been all those years ago. The bed. The flowery cover on it. The wardrobe. And that was where she would go now, that wardrobe. She'd sit inside it and drink the gin, then wait until she fell asleep for the last time.

Yes, that was what she'd do.

And maybe she'd think about Colin and what could have been while she was at it.

Colin couldn't shake the sense of foreboding that had come over him since he'd listened at Randall's office door. Something was off, and there wasn't anything he could do about it at the moment. But it didn't matter. Whatever it was would disappear along with them when he served their dinner.

He left his room and went into the kitchen to stir the meal he'd left braising in the slow cooker. He didn't care whether the bald gentleman liked stewed beef—that was what Colin and Randall would have had if Jackson hadn't turned up, so that was what they'd be having now. The food looked sufficiently tender, so he popped some new potatoes and carrots on the hob then walked over to the window while they came to the boil. Beside the window stood an old-fashioned cabinet, a Welsh dresser that had been there for as long as he could remember.

Back in the days when he'd first started work here, he'd been in charge of cleaning the pots. A deep white sink had been below the window then, the dresser beside it, and he'd stared across the fields as he'd washed up and thought of Nellie. It was strange how life worked out. He'd planned to marry her, to set up home and live happily ever after, get her a job in this house. But he'd gone to war and returned to hear from Matilda that Nellie

89

wasn't one for marriage, that she'd pledged to spend her life helping her mum and dad manage The Running Hare.

Colin had been upset, of course he had, but hadn't wanted anyone else. He'd resigned himself to always working in the house, and when his original masters had passed away and their children had employed him, he'd known he wouldn't go anywhere else. The children, as he still thought of them, had sold up, and Colin had worried about where he would go. But Randall had bought the place and kept him on—the sole employee who ran the house like clockwork.

He wondered whether Nellie ever thought of him. Perhaps he'd go down to the village tomorrow, after everything here had been settled, maybe visit with her for an hour or two before he jetted off into the sun. Who knew, perhaps she'd like to go with him. They could live the life they'd been denied.

Water sizzled on the hob, and he rushed over to turn down the heat. He tugged the bell cord dangling beside the cooker to let Randall know dinner would be ready in a bit. While he waited for the vegetables to cook, he returned to the dresser and took out some red wine. He uncorked it and reached deep into the dresser for a smaller bottle at the back. A few teaspoons of the contents poured into the wine would do the trick and, satisfied all was in order, he shuffled into the dining room to set the table.

A table for two.

Colin would eat in the kitchen, as he always did. He'd give it until he'd eaten his meal then go and investigate in the dining room. Things should have gone to plan nicely by that time. After that, the world would be his oyster.

CHAPTER ELEVEN

The butler had brought in an uncorked bottle of wine, but Randall had ignored it, saying they'd be better off sticking to water, considering what they'd be doing later. It wouldn't do them any good to be half cut from alcohol. Jackson had agreed.

"So, the deal with the butler?" Jackson pushed his plate aside and planted his elbows on the table. He laced his fingers and waited for Randall's response.

"Accident." He tapped beside his eye. "Protecting me."

"Ah, right. So he's always been protective, has he?"

"Just a bit." Randall smiled a tad. "He's been with me for a long time. Came with the house. Thinks he needs to take care of everything in it, even though he's thin and looks like he couldn't fight off a kid."

Randall rose then pushed his chair beneath the table. Jackson stood. He moved to collect the plates.

"The butler will do that." Randall nodded at the table.

"Right."

"Come on. I want to show you something." Randall moved to the door.

He led Jackson out of the dining room and upstairs, along the left-hand side of the veranda then through the third door into another hallway lined with doors. They walked down it, and right at the end was an ancient narrow staircase, bare stone walls either side. Frowning, because this hadn't been on the plans of the house he'd studied, Jackson trailed Randall upwards until they reached another door. Steel, which looked out of place in such a grand home.

Randall took a plastic card from his pocket and slid it down the middle of a black box on the jamb.

The loud click of bolts drawing across echoed in the small space and gave Jackson a momentary chill. It smelled funny up here—of years gone by, dust, and mould.

Randall pushed the door open to reveal a large circular room.

Jackson stepped inside. Going by what he could see, it was situated at the back of the house.

Windows, much like those in the control room of a lighthouse, allowed a bird's-eye view of the outside surroundings. Although the day had almost switched to night out there, Jackson could see well enough. If anyone came across those lawns they'd be spotted.

Opposite, below two of the windows, a bank of electronic paraphernalia with knobs, sliders, and lights drew his eye. It reminded him of music recording gear. It didn't fit here, was surreal and odd, and he frowned again, wondering what the hell tied this to Randall. Was the man some kind of performing artist?

Computer monitors—some square, black eyes of deadness, others alive and bright with streams of data rising from bottom to top—gave him pause. There was more to this man than he'd realised. More than Sid would have told him if he'd pushed for background information. All Jackson had thought was that this bloke had inherited this mansion, rattled around in it, wasting his days and playing about in life. First impressions had definitely been wrong on this occasion.

"What the hell is this room?" Jackson turned.

Randall closed the door and pressed a code into another keypad. "This is where I work. Where I come when I want to do a final check of the grounds at night. You'll note you can see in every direction."

"This doesn't do you any fucking good." Jackson lifted his hands then slapped them onto his outer thighs. "This room. It shows you sod all unless someone's on the grounds—someone you can see out of the windows. By the time you've made it downstairs, they could have got into the house and be waiting."

Randall jabbed another button. The sound of metal scraping metal clunked, much as it had when Randall had released the door locks.

"But they can't get in here." Randall smiled. "*This* could be classed as my panic room."

Jackson nodded. "You used it before for that purpose?"

"Yes. The last time someone came, I was in here for… I was in here."

"The butler didn't make it up here in time then. What's his name anyway?"

"Colin. I told him we had to come up here because I'd been alerted to someone being on the grounds. He said he could deal with it, and I believed him. He had a gun, after all. Had been in the army. I didn't want him to deal with it, wanted him to come up here with me so I could…sort things…but there was stuff I still needed to test in here, and it reminded me I couldn't afford to be killed."

What the hell do you do? Why couldn't you afford to be killed?

"What happened?" Jackson stared at a computer that bleeped an erratic, high-pitched alarm.

Randall frowned and walked over to it. He leant forward, pressed his hands to the desk, and studied the monitor, then pushed a button on the keyboard. A green image came up, similar to viewing something through night-vision goggles. A shape, dark and swiftly moving, was heading from the distance and into the foreground.

"Oh, some man stabbed Colin in the eye." Randall bit his bottom lip until it blanched white.

"And?" Jackson flicked his gaze from the screen to Randall then back again.

The shape had become the outline of a deer.

"And Colin killed him." Randall stared briefly at the ceiling as though offering up a prayer, then touched another button on the keyboard.

The deer buckled and fell to the ground.

He looked at Jackson. "That was a deer, and it was just inside the perimeter of my property. It worked. It bloody worked!" Randall raised his hands to his head and gripped his hair. He laughed a bit nutterishly then lowered his arms. "So your mention of this room doing no fucking good..."

"It alerted you to the deer when it had breached some sort of line?"

"Yes. And it was eliminated."

The deer was still on the ground. Unmoving.

"So this is some form of security as well as a killer of animals," Jackson said sarcastically, nodding at the computer.

"Yes. And before you ask, there are hidden screens in every room that I can access to check data like this as soon as my system spots it. That's how I knew the other person sent to kill me was on the property. I actually watched him run across the grounds and attempt to break into the east wing."

"That puts paid to me needing to give you a lecture on having gates and walls constructed then."

Randall smiled. "It does a bit, doesn't it? Of course, this alarm, for want of a better word, is still in the testing phase at the moment, but now it's killed something... Christ, I didn't think I'd crack it. My alarm, it isn't just an alarm."

I can fucking see that. Dread pooled in Jackson's belly. "So what is it?"

Randall chewed the inside of his cheek. "Something you really don't need to know about." He moved from the computers to a window that overlooked the rear of the house. "There had been information on the man who came for me, you know. In his pocket. A phone with contacts in it. A memory stick with data on it. Which is how I knew someone would be arriving tonight to finish off what they'd started—several future dates if that first one didn't work. It was all there. The dates and times of 'jobs', much like Sid has, I suspect."

Jackson nodded. "You'd have thought whoever it was would have known to change those dates and times once they'd realised their man and their information wasn't coming back." He joined Randall at the window, wondering where the hell the man was who'd come to kill Randall last time. Had Colin disposed of the body?

"You would think that, yes." Randall stared out of one of the windows. "But the person who wants me killed hadn't banked on Colin dragging the dead man into his car and delivering the body back to him. Or onto the property of his private residence, anyway. Complete with data, as though we hadn't even seen it."

"So I take it you copied it then?" *Colin? Dragging a bloke? With one of his eyes hanging out?* He couldn't imagine, wiry and weak-looking as the man was, that he'd been able to do what he had. He must have been in some considerable pain. Maybe Colin had got rid of him the next day. Maybe... *Don't ask about it. Just don't ask.*

"I did copy it, yes. I still have it should you need to see it, although I doubt you do since Sid is kindly taking care of the main problem while we take care of the other later."

We?

"Right. So, the main *problem* hasn't got anyone who'll take over where he left off?"

"Sadly, he does. Knowing him, he'll have it written down in code somewhere that he wants his son killed even after he's dead."

"What?" Jackson widened his eyes. "Your fucking *dad* wants you dead and you're prepared for him to be killed?"

"Yes, I am, and of *course* he wants me dead." A faint smile touched Randall's lips, showing sadness. "I'm a bastard."

Jackson held back a wry chuckle. This just kept getting better.

You're in way over your head, Hiscock.

"Oh, fuck me. Does this shit still go on?" Jackson was surprised. "Do snobs still want their illegitimate children out of the picture so badly they'd have them killed?"

"Seems so. I'm not about to tell everyone who I am, who he is to me, but he can't take that chance. He's...well known. According to him, I could ruin his political future." Randall laughed quietly. "What he doesn't realise is that I don't *care* about his political future. I want no part of it or his life. I just want to live here in peace, to study, to work, but then I'm on the verge of being well known myself. He knows that. I've heard it frightens him. He wants something from me, yet he doesn't want me knowing he has it. Having me killed, my software stolen, would mean he could have what he wants without the fear of me letting anyone know he has it."

Jackson was confused as fuck, and it was on the tip of his tongue to ask Randall to explain what he was going on about, but he changed his mind. "What *exactly* do you do?" He gestured at the computers.

"I've developed certain software over the years, hence me having enough money to own this house. I don't like this place much, just bought it because I could, because it meant beating my father in the bid for it. I wanted him to see he couldn't have everything he wanted. Childish, but something I felt I had to do at the time. And now?" He rubbed a palm over his stubble. "Now I have new software that many people want. There's an underground bidding war going on over it, apparently."

Jackson swivelled to stare out of the window again. "Right. And that software is?"

Randall closed his eyes. "I told you earlier that I needed someone I trusted because of...secrets. Well, this is my secret. This room and everything in it. My work..." He paused. "My work nearly wasn't complete, ready for tonight, and I thought it wasn't until that deer was killed. If I'd known it would work, my latest tweaks, you wouldn't even need to be here." He sighed.

"What is this software? Why wouldn't I need to be here?"

The penny dropped, but before Jackson could say anything, Randall blinked then faced him.

"It would have killed the intruder for me."

Jackson wanted to laugh. This was the shit of movies, fantastical crap. Yeah, he knew there were things out there that the average person wasn't aware of, but something that would have killed a man, something that was governed by a computer?

It happens, you know it happens. It's just that seeing it when the software is in someone's house and not in a war situation... It's thrown you off, that's all.

"How?" Jackson asked.

Randall shrugged. "That's a part of my secret you'll never know. But I will tell you the man won't make it to the house. Like that deer there"—he jerked a thumb at the monitor—"he'll only need to step onto the grounds and he'll be taken care of if that's where I choose for him to die." He thumped his fist against the window as though trying to contain his excitement.

Jackson should have been alarmed. Should have thought Randall a crazy bastard, but he didn't. "I see. And if the software works later?" he asked.

"I'll become a murderer."

"And if you sell it?"

"I'll be a killer several times over, I imagine, even though I personally will never have killed a soul."

CHAPTER TWELVE

Colin wasn't best pleased. He'd stupidly allowed himself to have a little nap, thinking no one would be any the wiser because Randall and that bald man were probably well out of the picture by now. He went into the dining room, expecting to find Randall and that grim-looking fellow sprawled on the floor, having fallen off their chairs, drugged and out of it. No such sight greeted him. He spotted the full wine bottle immediately, the still-clean glasses, and cursed under his breath.

"I'm going to have to explain to my boss why I failed. That I fell asleep, of all things."

He glanced at his watch. The two hours his boss had given him were well and truly up. He quickly cleared away the dinner things, dumping them onto the drainer beside the kitchen sink, then retrieved the wine and poured it down the plughole. If he tried to get them to drink it now, he'd alert them, get them all suspicious.

No, Colin would have to let things progress as they would have before he'd offered to get rid of Randall and his new friend. He'd rethink, perhaps let that Jackson man kill the person being sent here later. Let Randall think Colin had nothing to do with any of this mess. Then Colin could hand his notice in—tomorrow morning would be a good time—saying he'd been kept awake all night thinking and that working for Randall had now become too much. At his age, he couldn't risk anything too stressful. With Randall being sympathetic, Colin could perhaps shoot him in the back before leaving the property, never to return. Never to live in this country again.

Yes, and he'd definitely pop into the village to drop in on Nellie.

He felt better for having a purpose, a new plan in place now his previous one had gone wrong. He went into his room, unsurprised that his phone was vibrating. Answered it. Listened to what was being said.

"But they didn't want wine with dinner, sir," he said. "So your man needs to visit after all."

"I had a feeling you'd mess this up, Colin."

"I'm terribly sorry, sir." He gritted his teeth.

"It can't be helped. So long as everything is squared away by the morning... Then you need to scarper. The funds will be deposited into your bank. But before you go, make sure to leave his top room unlocked."

"I will, sir."

"This should be the last time we speak."

"Indeed. Goodbye."

The phone clicked without a tarra or a Godspeed in return. Colin was oddly distraught by that. It was plain manners, surely, that his boss should thank him or wish him well. After all he'd done, keeping an eye on Randall...

He went into the little room behind his. He wanted to make sure the hidden screen there was in full working order. Then he'd check on Randall and Jackson. Let them know he was available to them should he be needed. Actually, he'd insist he wanted to be present. This time he didn't want to risk anything going wrong. Not when he was so close to getting to that beach, that paradise in the sun.

CHAPTER THIRTEEN

Back in the vast lounge, Jackson sat on one of the sofas, leaning forward with his head in his hands. While Randall was in his study checking the main system that linked to his computers upstairs, Jackson tried to work out what the hell kind of software had the ability to kill someone. He came up with maybe an electrical force field being issued, bullets or silent bombs being set off, the kind of shit that already existed out there. He decided he didn't want to know what Randall had been working on, that if it were something that would be sold to countries who chose to use it for mass murder and the like, he'd be better off in the dark.

Come on. Mass murder? That's a bit much. Isn't it?

As they'd left that circular room and made their way downstairs, Randall had said, "If I'd known the software was completely ready, the man coming tonight would have been taken care of, then would have just simply disappeared. You wouldn't have needed to know anything about this. I'm sorry that you do, because it might bother you when you leave here, but at the same time, I'm not. I'm glad I got to share a part of me with someone who...who understands that killing is sometimes necessary."

Jackson hadn't answered—what the fuck was there to say to that?—but it played on his mind now, even though he was trying to block it out. And if the software had the capability to kill someone who had just happened to step onto the outskirts of the property... No, it couldn't be gas. It had to be some form of weapon.

He huffed out a laugh as his imagination ran riot, conjuring bullets tipped with poison.

I'm in neck deep...

The swish of the door opening had Jackson looking up.

Randall had returned and walked towards him. "Are you all right?"

Jackson turned his head to face him. "You'd prefer honesty, yeah?"

Randall nodded.

"No, I'm not all right. A part of me wants to know what the hell you're up to, but another part?" He shook his head. "Jesus, I don't want to know. See, I kill people, I explained all that, but when I'm doing it, I'm getting rid of a bad person."

"As I will be tonight if everything has come together as it should have and the software doesn't hit a glitch."

"Yeah, and I get that. But this *selling* of the software? Bugs the fuck out of me. How can you be sure you'd be selling it to the right person? Or what if that person sells it on to someone else? Someone bad? You mentioned a bidding war, but what if the one with the most money wins—you'd sell to them, right?—and that winner has a different use for the software to what you intended? What then?"

"That's been my issue for a long time, since the idea of the software came along. I developed it for my own personal use, then got stupid and wanted to tell people about it. To share what I'd done because it was so bloody amazing. I put the word out there on a secret forum that it would soon be finished, and I knew it would be wanted by many—after all, who doesn't want to quietly eliminate people who want to eliminate them? It was meant for people in my situation. A covert acquiring of the software for those in the know.

109

They could obtain the alarm system and software and it would keep them from harm. But others found out about it."

"Others?"

"People in various governments."

"Oh shit. Didn't you *realise* they would once word got out?"

"Clearly, I didn't think. My need to be recognised somehow overtook common sense. Although the information was put out there without my name being mentioned—I did it via my computer, used an alias—I knew it wouldn't take an expert long to track it back to me, even though I took preventative measures." He shook his head. "And it *was* tracked back. By my father—or someone working for him. I should have known they would have some kind of monitor on my computer anyway. They probably have all the data and now just need the actual software to run it from."

He paused, biting his lower lip. "So, despite tonight and my immediate threats being taken care of, I may possibly gain more threats in the future if my father has told other people I'm the one who created the software. I shouldn't have let the word out. Shouldn't have been so damn needy for recognition." He went quiet, then added, "Shouldn't have wanted to show him I was worth something—that even though I was a bastard, we could... Fuck it."

"Look, I get that, I really do, mate, but what's done is done, and we need to deal with clearing this shit up. If this software is so good... They think it's complete, do they? The people who know it exists, I mean."

Randall nodded.

"So what kind of nutter would risk coming here to take it from you when they know it's set up here, when they know what it can do?"

"Because some people want it very badly and would be prepared to risk lives to get it. Why do you think my father sent that last man here? Why do you think he set up a bloody timetable of return visits if previous ones didn't work out? Because he knew the men he was sending to kill me, sending to get the software, would die."

"Then you shouldn't be here! If he has people in his employ like you, who know what they're doing, who are able to figure out just from your data how it works, they'll be working on ways to dodge being killed, to shut down your system in order to seize your software. They don't have to be on your property to have your electricity supply stopped. I'm assuming there needs to be a steady supply for your software to work?"

"Yes. Generators come in handy there."

Jackson shook his head and stared at the coffee table. "So no matter what they try, providing your generators don't pack up, you'd be safe from them."

"Pretty much. I wouldn't have been, but that deer going down…"

"And say they got through, got to the house somehow. What then?"

"The software… I think I'm there with it."

"So I'm just here in case your software doesn't work?" Jackson got up and walked to the window he'd watched Sid through earlier. Anger burned inside him. If the software was basically complete, if there was something else that could kill the assassin instead of him...

"You do understand why I needed you here, don't you?" Randall asked.

Jackson did, but it didn't mean he liked being used. Then another thought struck him. What did it matter anyway? He was being paid, wasn't he? He'd been employed to do a job. Whether or not he ended up doing it was neither here nor there—he'd get paid anyway. Sid had already been given the money. He didn't need to know *how* their visitor had got killed, just that he was dead. And Jackson doubted Randall would be telling Sid his secret. Jackson would tell Sid he'd dealt with the body, so no one would be any the wiser.

"Yeah, I get it," Jackson said. "I'd prefer it if I could just do the honours then leave, not have to witness you trying out whatever it is you need to try out." He turned to face Randall. "But if it gets the job done..."

"Hopefully it will. What better person to do a final test on than someone who's coming here to kill me? Someone who's going to be killed anyway?"

Jackson tried to read whether madness lurked behind the man's eyes. He didn't see any. Nothing but the pleading for understanding. "I s'pose." He nodded. "Yep, I think I can work with that. How...? What will you be setting off?"

"I already told you—you don't need to know." Randall smiled.

"I think I fucking do if it puts me in the firing line, don't you?"

"It doesn't. It won't."

"There's a problem with your software," Jackson said. "Unless you've thought of it already. What if someone buys it for protection and ends up setting it off and it kills an innocent person? What if some bloke who lives in a built-up area has it and the postman walks up the path and cops it? Or a kid out playing? Some girl skipping, laughing with her friends? What then?"

"The people who would have this software would generally live remotely like I do. It doesn't come cheap. And it doesn't kill people automatically. You have to press a button."

"But what about the snobs, the stars who live in those multi-million-pound villas, all in a row at Sandbanks, wherever the fuck that is? I can't see one of their friends being killed by accident going down too well, can you? If they're just a figure on screen and they press that button... This is what I was saying before. You sell this to the wrong person, and it might well end up exactly like I just described. This is dangerous shit. You should scrap it, pretend you never created it."

"I should, you're right."

"Then why don't you?"

"I don't know. I just can't let it go. Not until I've seen it work on that man."

"Right. So you test it tonight, and if it works you'll be happy? Like whatever it was that drove

113

you to create it in the first place will be satisfied that the job's complete?"

"I hope that'll be the case. That would solve a lot of future problems."

"If I were you, I'd test it then destroy the whole thing. You've opened a nasty can of worms here, letting governments know such a thing exists. They won't rest until they have your system, you know that, don't you?"

Randall sniffed. "If I decide to destroy it, people would want me to tell them how they could recreate it. I'd have to go into hiding. Always running."

"Damn straight you would. What the hell made you *do* this?"

He shouldn't have asked, hadn't really needed to. This bloke had been more afraid of his father than he'd wanted to admit. Jackson would know soon enough who that man was. If he was as prominent as Randall had implied, his death would be all over the news come the morning. For Randall—for *anyone*—to have the need to create something so...so outrageous to protect himself, he had to have been frightened for his life. Had to have been threatened, to have believed the threats.

Who the fuck is *his father?*

"I rather thought you would have realised why I did this," Randall said.

"Yeah, I do, but come on! Sid—"

"I started my research before I knew about companies like Sid's. I had to protect myself. My

114

world isn't like yours. My father... Once he found out about me, it all started. Small things."

"Like what?"

Randall shrugged. "People accosting me in the city, telling me I would disappear soon if I didn't disappear by myself. That kind of thing."

"Why not just get out of your dad's range?"

"Because he would have found me wherever I went. And even with him gone, if he's left instructions... They'll find me wherever I go after tonight."

"Unless you get a new identity. Move away. Sid knows people who can make it seem like you never existed."

Randall walked to the sofa and flopped down casually, as though what they'd been discussing wasn't a matter of life or death, of subterfuge and crime-riddled dealings. Yeah, Jackson knew this kind of thing went on, but it was usually between governments, as far as he'd been aware, or those in the underground crime rings.

But it is to do with governments.

He shook his head, having to admit now that there were covert outfits he'd heard about but hadn't fully believed were real. Outfits who had men at their disposal who thought nothing of threatening men like Randall on the street. In his own home.

Why didn't you believe they were around? You work for Sid, you dickhead. He's the same kind of outfit. Christ Almighty...

Jackson had buried his head in the sand, going about as though his job wasn't anything to write home about. Pretending that killing people didn't hurt anyone. Yeah, he knew deep down he wrecked lives, but he hadn't allowed himself to *really* think about it. Now, here, Randall had yanked Jackson's head up out of that sand, and Jackson was left with the gritty taste of the beach in his mouth—as though all those he'd killed were wet dust on his tongue, returning to choke him for what he'd done.

CHAPTER FOURTEEN

Langham woke, cold, the room in total darkness. He glanced at his watch—eleven p.m.—wide awake.

Shit.

He padded over to the window. Looked out onto the street. There was activity out there—he hadn't expected anything less. A couple of uniformed officers milled about on the path.

Something was going on at The Running Hare. Fairbrother must have got inside—or got the old woman to open the door at any rate. Several police vehicles were in the car park, left at random angles, as though they'd arrived in haste, the officers needing to get inside quickly. He leant on the sill, hands flat, arms ramrod straight, and contemplated going down there for a nose. What kind of help could he even be anyway? They'd have everything under control. He wasn't needed.

Curiosity gripped him, though. He wouldn't be able to get back to sleep. He got ready and, keys in pocket, left the room. In the lobby, an officer, the one from earlier, was stationed there. Langham walked outside. The fresh air slapped him hard, and if any remnants of sleep had had a mind to hang about, they fucked off then. He stood there, chilled, shivering, and thrust his hands into his trousers pockets. Made for The Running Hare.

The sign swung in the breeze, one that had picked up in its intensity since the last time he'd been out here. Something about that sign still bothered him and, once he got to the car park, he kept away from it, convinced it would lift itself off its hanger and throw itself at him. As he approached the main door, Fairbrother was on his way out, a bit green around the gills, despite being a seasoned officer.

"What the fuck are you doing here?" Fairbrother sniffed in a huge lungful of air.

"Couldn't sleep." Langham shrugged. "You know how it is."

"Yep, but I reckon you'd be better off going back to where you came from, mate. This shit's got a damn sight worse since I spoke to you last."

Langham frowned. "Why? Playing you up, is she?"

"Nope, we're searching for her now. She may well have done a runner, considering the mess in there."

Langham was going to go inside without an invite. He had to see the *mess* for himself. "I'll go and have a look, shall I?"

"If you have to, but you'll probably regret it. I've come out here for a breath of fresh air. It's just inside there, and not only that, shit's going on out the back."

Langham frowned again. Grabbed some protectives and suited up. Went inside. Was assaulted by the grim sight of a man who had once sipped Guinness in his ratty chair—a man whose head had been caved in, and the only reason Langham knew it was the old man was because he recognised his clothes.

Someone had given him quite a battering, and Langham found it difficult to imagine the old woman doing this. Then again, she'd had a bit of a mad glint in her eyes earlier, when they'd come back here to collect their things. And she wasn't a spindly little thing, incapable of hurting someone. But to inflict this kind of damage? That was a lot of rage. The dead man may as well have had no head. It had been walloped so many times the skull had split, then bits of it had broken away. Knowing the strength of skull bone and how much force was needed to cave a head in, Langham realised she'd been beyond angry—at the seeing red stage. Hurt had to have been behind this attack, perhaps years of upset and suffering coming to the fore, giving her the strength to render this man facially unrecognisable. And fear. If she had thought she was going to get caught for killing the lady over the road…

"Jesus fucking wept." He covered his mouth with his wrist.

Blood spatter had sprayed quite a distance, the majority of it dried, or drying farthest away from the victim, but the area immediately surrounding him was still tacky. Thick in places. The man's clothing was soaked with it. The old woman had to have been covered, and if she hadn't washed before she'd left, someone would have spotted her, given the state she'd have been in.

Where is she?

"You searched this place?" he asked a young officer standing near the bottom of the stairs.

"Yes, sir."

"Right." He walked out the back, alarmed that forensic tents had been erected while he'd slept.

What the hell?

Fairbrother joined him. "Grim business, eh? We noticed the earth had been disturbed out here, and one of the new lads had a bit of a look and found a bone sticking up out of the ground."

"A bone?"

"Yep. Seems the old girl—or that fella in there—likes killing people. Quite a few bones have been found so far—more than one person, definitely a man and a woman. There might be others. You know, buried deeper."

"I knew something was off about her, but bloody hell!"

"We've searched this place once, but I've sent men upstairs again. Loads of nooks and crannies in a gaff like this. I'd say she's long gone, but you never know, do you."

"No." Langham took a few seconds to process things. Who the hell was buried out here? And why had they even been killed? Shit, he was glad this wasn't his case. There were too many loose ends that needed tying up.

Back inside, he stood as far away from the victim as he could so he didn't contaminate the scene. Stared around, trying to think of where she could have gone. The attic would have already been checked, as would the rooms, but...

A smudge of blood caught his attention, on the wall beside the stairs. Like a thumb print that had been dragged downwards. He walked towards it, examined farther up. Faint, bloody fingerprints, as if someone had needed to touch the wall for balance in order to even make it up the stairs.

"Fairbrother!" he shouted.

The thud of running feet on wooden flooring sounded, then Fairbrother was beside Langham.

"See those?" Langham asked.

"Fuck."

Fairbrother took the lead, going up the stairs two by two. Langham followed, careful not to touch the walls. Fairbrother stared at those on the landing then went up another flight, one that was narrower and possibly led to the private quarters. A large swipe of pink blood was on the wall beside a door, as though clothing had pressed against it. Fairbrother walked in, and Langham peered over his shoulder—a bedside cabinet door open, nothing inside it. Another impression of blood on the doorjamb. Why the fuck hadn't the officers followed this or even seen it?

"She's been up here all right," Fairbrother said. "And heads are going to fucking roll. Even I missed this. Shit."

"Let's just find her—don't worry about it." Langham left the room and moved down the hallway to another door that had blood on the threshold. "In here!"

A double bed, like something out of the past with its ancient bedspread. Time hadn't moved on. Oddly, considering the amount of blood clues up to this point so far, this room didn't appear to have any inside. Something clonked, and Langham cocked his head, trying to work out where the noise had come from.

"You do the honours," he said to Fairbrother, nodding at a built-in cupboard.

Langham stood back and waited in case the woman burst out and barrelled into them. Fairbrother crept to the cupboard and looked like he wished he were anywhere but there. He tugged on the small handle, and the door creaked open.

Langham held his breath, his stomach contents souring, but no one charged out, no one screeched or attacked.

The cupboard seemed deep—and dark.

Fairbrother produced a torch, flicked it on, then shone it inside.

Langham moved closer. The old woman sat on the floor, her cheek on her shoulder, as though she were just taking a nap. Blood covered her clothes, her hair clumped with it, and a bottle of some description was on the floor beside her. It rocked—*must have been what that clonk was*—and vomit, thick and lumpy, coated the fabric of her top over one breast.

"She dead?" Langham asked.

Fairbrother stepped back. "D'you want to be the one to find out? Fucked if I want to touch her."

Langham swallowed. Picked up a small compact mirror off the dresser. Took Fairbrother's torch and stepped into the cupboard, bracing himself for the woman to wake up, see him, and freak the fuck out. He went up close, holding the mirror beneath her nose, pointing the torch beam at her face. Her skin had a greenish pallor, the wrinkles somehow grey at the edges. Her eyes were closed, and crusts of blood had lifted from her face, on the verge of drifting away.

He concentrated on his task. Held his breath.

No mist on the mirror.

"She's long gone, I think." Langham put the mirror in the hand he held the torch with. He breathed through his mouth, battling the urge to be sick, and took her wrist in hand so he could check for a pulse. Didn't find one. "Yep, gone."

He stepped out of the cupboard. Released a sigh—one of relief that he wasn't in such a confined space with a once-crazy old woman. The stench was also getting to him—alcohol-laced vomit wasn't one of the better things he'd smelt.

"We've got to be bloody mad," Langham said, "to do this job."

"You have," Fairbrother said. "You're on holiday, yet still you're willing to get in there with a blood-covered, sick-riddled old woman. Something wrong with you, mate."

Langham nodded. "Maybe."

Or maybe I'm just married to my fucking job. Maybe I've just been pretending, kidding myself that I can take a break and forget it for a while. Trying to be someone I'm not—someone who can walk away from what's a part of him.

The thoughts bothered him so much he left the room, going into the bar to ask for a statement pad. He scribbled down what had happened since he'd got here. When Fairbrother appeared again, Langham handed it over.

"Here's my statement. Saves holding your paperwork up while I'm in Spain or wherever we end up going—you know, you waiting for me to get back and whatever. I need to get away from here. I should never have come out."

"I did wonder," Fairbrother said. "But thanks all the same. For, you know…"

"Like I said, don't worry about it. She's found now. No one needs to know she was missed the first time or that I arrived after the initial search." He raised his hand in farewell and stepped past the cordon that had been erected around the old man.

Outside, he sucked in some much-needed fresh air. A shiver ran through him, and an image of the old woman in the cupboard loomed in his mind. He glanced at the swinging sign. Shuddered and hunched his shoulders to try to stop the gusts of wind sneaking down his shirt collar. He walked to Simmons'. Went straight upstairs, knocked on Oliver's door.

Oliver opened it, his hair tousled, face flushed. "There are several people in a strawberry patch out the back of the pub."

"Yep, bones have been found."

"She did them all in, you know. The old woman," Oliver said.

"Yep, nutty as a fucking fruitcake, that one."

"I got the sense her head was broken," Oliver said.

Hers wasn't the only one... "Yep, she can't have been right up top. And if you know why she did it, maybe leave it until we get back from abroad before you report it in? I've just found the batty old bird in a cupboard of all places. Seems like she killed a bloke—caved his head in with a poker by the looks of it—then must have taken some pills or something. Had a bottle of booze in there, and she'd puked on herself. May well have brought up a load of tablets but choked on her vomit. Possibly suffocated. I don't know, but I can't wait to get out of here. Get the hell away."

CHAPTER FIFTEEN

With Randall's revelations, clarity had come. Jackson would have preferred that clarity to have hit him after the kill, once he'd returned home. He could flounder in it then, chastise himself for being so stupid in thinking his current line of business was what kept Christine's betrayal at bay. That his work was what made everything all right again. But it blared at him now, that he'd been pretending, making out this was who he was and that was that. All a load of bullshit. Yeah, he'd killed bad people—and if it wasn't him doing it, someone else on Sid's team would—but shit, how could he have ever believed killing them meant killing Christine and what she'd done? Where was the logic in that? He'd be classed as fucking crazy if he ever went for counselling.

But heartbreak meant things appeared differently, it seemed. Having his heart broken justified his actions. Or so he'd thought. Jackson had grabbed on to that way of thinking instead of facing his shit—instead of facing Christine and telling her exactly what he thought of her before he'd returned to the war and found himself a changed man.

Still, the past was done, wasn't a damn thing he could do about it now. After tonight, he could do what he should have done a long time ago. Admit that maybe Christine had been lonely and had reached out for another man because missing Jackson had been too much. Or that she wasn't who he'd thought she was. Yeah, that was more like it. Jackson had fallen for someone who didn't have the same values, who hadn't meant it when she'd said she loved him. Jackson had seen and believed what he'd wanted to, because it had made him feel good, it had felt right. If he thought about it properly, the signs had been there. Christine's letters may have contained the right words, but the feeling hadn't come across in the last few months like it had before. If Jackson read them now he'd see it—see those words as bland, something just written as a duty, to fob him off and get him thinking everything was okay back home.

Maybe Christine hadn't wanted to end it while he'd been away fighting. Or maybe, just maybe, what with the cruel way it *had* ended, Christine was a bitch and had orchestrated it that way, had *wanted* to see the pain in his eyes. To punish him for ever leaving her in the first place, even though she'd known he'd been a soldier right from the off.

Some people are like that. No rhyme or reason.

Jackson acknowledged he'd become like his ex-lover on that fateful day he'd caught her in bed with that young bloke. Expressing no genuine feelings of love, going about with a sneer because it was easier to put on a mask and be someone else. He'd raked in the cash to prove he could do this thing called life by himself.

And now he wanted to be who he really was. Jackson, a man who had a lot to give to the right person.

He paced the lounge while Randall was in his study. He glanced at his watch. Midnight. Time had crawled by since they'd last talked, and Jackson had stayed in this room in order to give Randall space. Time to think about whether he'd destroy the software, keep it active in his home to remain safe, or sell it on. A life on the run wasn't something he thought Randall could cope with either, but if he let Sid take care of things, set him up with a new identity, he wouldn't be running. He'd be someone else entirely.

It wasn't too late to walk away.

Jackson left the lounge and walked to the study. The door was ajar, and he peeped through the crack, viewing one half of Randall from the back. His hair had been gathered into a low ponytail. Jackson contemplated returning to the lounge and waiting for Randall to join him.

"I know you're there," Randall said. "Saw you coming."

Of course he had. The alarm would have told him someone was up and about. Colin had retired to his rooms, although he'd said he'd come out once three a.m. neared. Jackson had told him he wasn't needed, but the old man wouldn't hear of it.

"I was here for Randall the first time, sir," Colin had said. "And I'll be here again."

Very noble of him—or stupid. Still, this time the man wouldn't lose an eye, wouldn't lose anything if Jackson could prevent it.

"Why don't you come in?" Randall asked.

"Because you're busy."

"I was, but I've gone through the data on the main computer in my upstairs room and I'm sure everything is set now. It's as ready as it'll ever be." Randall didn't turn around, didn't swivel in his chair to lift an arm and beckon Jackson in. He remained hunched over, gaze undoubtedly glued to the monitor.

Jackson pushed the door and went inside. Closed it behind him. He approached the desk but stopped a few feet away. The man might not want him to see what was on the monitor, which appeared to be a screen full of random numbers and symbols. Nothing he'd be able to decipher, but that code had to have taken a lot of work, and Randall might be protective of it.

Randall pressed a button, and the code disappeared, replaced by the eerie, night-vision-like image of something outside. Jackson couldn't make it out.

"Grab that spare chair and come and sit by me," Randall said.

Jackson sat on Randall's left. He wanted to be the one who was closest to the door.

"You see this here?" Randall touched the screen with his fingertip.

Jackson squinted, leaning forward. Nothing but a dark rectangle filling the bottom half of the screen and a lighter one above.

"That's out there." Randall nodded to the window opposite. "If you look closely, you'll see a rabbit."

Jackson blinked then concentrated harder. Nope. No rabbit. Then he caught a quick glimpse of two eyes, as though a streak of light had gone across them, lime green one second then gone the next. "All right..."

"Now watch this." Randall tapped the keyboard, and a grey circle with a cross in the centre came up over the original image.

Oh Jesus...

He knew what was going to happen, and as much as he didn't want to, he couldn't stop staring.

It's no different from someone hunting. No damn different.

131

Randall pressed another key, and the lighting on the screen changed to a brighter hue. A flash. Now the rabbit's outline was clearly visible, its ears perked, the animal up on its hind legs. Another jab of a button, and the rabbit keeled over. Jackson shook his head, astounded by how fast it had happened. What the hell had killed it? Had to have been a bullet. But where were the guns? He hadn't noticed anything odd about the exterior when he and Sid had arrived, but then again, he hadn't particularly taken much notice. That was supposed to have come later, him doing a scout around the property. Why poke about outside when hidden cameras could do it for you?

"The cameras are set in tiny recesses in the outer walls," Randall said. "Thought I'd better answer that question before you asked it. They're not visible to the casual observer, although I expect you would have noticed the holes had you looked."

Jackson could have taken that as an admonishment but chose instead to take it for what it was—just a casual bit of conversation. "Listen, I've been thinking. I touched on this earlier, but if you could get away—right now, tonight—and start a new life, would you?"

Randall turned to face him. "If this works, kills that man, I suppose I could. But going now, right now? Without knowing if it was strong enough to kill a person? No. It would bug me, the not knowing. I need to make sure I haven't been chasing rainbows the past few years. I have to know I'm right, that I've completed something."

Jackson could understand that but was buggered if he'd stay around if he were in Randall's shoes. Too many people would be on his arse—even after tonight they'd be dogging him—and to stick around just to finish a project, knowing his life was in danger?

Fuck that.

Jackson shrugged. "You seeing what I see?"

"Bastards have sent him early," Randall said.

Randall hovered one hand over his keyboard, that hand shaking. This was the moment of truth, the time he got to find out whether years of work had been worth it. Jackson couldn't imagine how he felt, knowing that even if it worked, he might as well not have bothered creating it in the first place—assuming Randall did what he'd said he would and destroyed the software afterwards.

Jackson leant forward, stared at the monitor. Randall pushed a button and brought the image of a figure up closer. Yes, it was definitely a man, someone dressed in black, in a balaclava or some kind of head gear.

"Fuck me," Jackson said. "Press the damn button."

"I just wanted to check it wasn't an innocent," Randall said. He let out an unsteady breath.

Button pressed.

The man went down like a sack of shit. Randall zoomed in closer, prodded another button or two, and a red and yellow splodge came up in the middle of the screen, like the camera had switched to one that sought out heat.

"I can't see a heart beating, can you?" Jackson inspected the screen, calm as you like.

"I can't see anything but a heap of red and yellow," Jackson said.

A knock sounded on the door, and Jackson jumped up, annoyed with himself for having been so entranced. This could have been a trap—the man out there could have been a decoy.

Fuck it.

He put his finger to his lips then moved to the door, withdrawing his gun. He snatched the door open, immediately in a shooting position.

Colin stood there.

"I saw something on one of your TVs, sir," he said to Randall. "A rabbit. It reminded me of the one on the pub sign in the village. Then there was another shape, like a man was on the grounds."

"Yes," Randall said. "No need to worry, Colin. He won't be bothering us."

Colin puffed his chest out. "My goodness, sir, then we must go outside and make sure he still isn't a threat. Make doubly sure he won't be bothering us."

If the old man wanted to play the hero, Jackson wasn't going to stop him.

"Sorry," Jackson said. "But Randall isn't going anywhere. Not until I've checked the area."

Colin smiled, his lips forming an eerie, wonky slash. He raised his hand. Narrowed his eyes.

A gunshot sounded, loud and disturbing.

Jackson winced.

Colin stared.

Randall shouted something.

And Jackson had just been pissed the hell off.

Colin couldn't quite work out why he was on the floor. He'd pulled his gun on that Jackson fellow, wanting to eradicate him then Randall in short time and get away while he had the chance. Instead, he stared at the ceiling, which appeared to be darkening. Were the lights being dimmed?

"What the fuck?" the bald man said to his left. "What the hell were you *thinking*, you weird old bastard?"

Colin wanted to answer that he'd intended on killing them, but his mouth didn't seem to work anymore. His chest hurt, too, just below his heart, and he struggled to suck in a decent amount of air. It came to him then, why he was on the floor, why he had pain. That slaphead guest had shot *him* instead.

I should have known. I did know. Knew he was better than your average killer.

He thought about his boss, wishing the phone he'd been given could be used to ring out. He could have called him now, even if he couldn't speak, so his boss would know something was wrong when Jackson and Randall spoke.

But I doubt he'd even care.

The thought was sobering, and Colin had the strange, unsettling feeling that his life hadn't amounted to much in the end. Just a sad man who'd pledged to serve people living in this house—and for what? To end up a corpse on an office floor?

He smiled. And his mouth must have decided to work because he laughed.

"What's so bloody funny?" Randall snapped. "I don't see what's so amusing, Colin. I thought you were on my side. The last time someone came here you lost an eye protecting me. What changed?"

Colin laughed harder.

The bald man, that Jackson, cleared his throat. "Listen, I've killed people, you know that, and after tonight I'd decided I wasn't going to do it anymore—I was going to fuck off somewhere, start again. But him?" He pointed at Colin. "He knows things, could get you in the shit." He paused. "You need to make some decisions. You need to get rid of him."

"I do?" Randall said.

It seemed Randall cared for him to some degree. He'd sounded alarmed at what Jackson had suggested.

Jackson bent over Colin, obliterating the sight of the ceiling. His strong-boned face held an expression of menace, something that churned Colin's stomach with immeasurable amounts of fear. Colin stopped laughing. The glint in the man's eyes—he didn't like it.

"I'll take him outside," Jackson said. "He won't be going anywhere fast, what with the state of him. Then I'll come back. Then you'll press that button. Kill him. After that, it's time for us to leave."

Randall sighed. Nodded.

136

Colin smiled. Typical. Randall would probably go and live the life Colin had planned. Beaches. Bars. Warm seas. Sun loungers. Cocktails with cherries and paper umbrellas. No worries. Every day full of nothing but wonderment.

Still, what did it matter now? The pain below his heart was increasing, and shortly he'd be dead. All that would be left after they'd disposed of him was any blood staining the floor. He closed his eye, wanted to poke his nail into the skin of his missing one. Didn't have the energy. He was picked up in strong arms, and he thought of Nellie. Thought of the picture on the pub sign and how he was going to end up like that rabbit outside earlier.

The image of that sign told him that fate had twinned him and Nellie right from the start. Maybe they *were* meant to be together. It was just a shame he had to wait a while in Hell before he'd see her again. But come to think of it, she'd go to Heaven, his Nellie, he was sure of that, so they wouldn't get to see one another after all.

A shame, that.

CHAPTER SIXTEEN

Since coming to Marsh Vines, Langham hadn't had the chance to forget work at all, and now fatigue overcame him, except he didn't want to sleep here. He just wanted to get the hell away. "Want to go home?"

"Yep."

"Come on. I just need my own fucking bed now."

Langham led the way down to the foyer. He had a hunch that if they stayed and came into contact with officers tomorrow, he'd end up staying put and helping them out. After signing out of the register, he made for the car, pleased once he was putting their bags in the boot. He should never have ignored his instincts when they'd first arrived. And their arrival seemed like days ago, yet it had just been hours. If he'd kept on driving, gone through the village instead of stopping… If he hadn't seen Sid Mondon and Jackson Hiscock, the first indication that their holiday wasn't going to turn out as a holiday after all…

Once in the car, he started the engine then whacked up the heat. Drove away from a village he never wanted to go to again. And what *was* it with villages lately? Supposedly quiet places where nothing ever happened. In his experience, that was turning out to be a load of crap.

"That place," he said, glancing across at Oliver, "was weird."

"It was, but there's a weirder place up ahead." Oliver balanced his elbow on the door then propped his face in his hand. Stared into the darkness, narrowing his eyes.

Oh fuck. "What do you mean?"

The last thing Langham wanted was more weirdness, more offences encroaching on his time. He fought the urge to shout, to go on a rant about just needing a bit of bloody peace, for fuck's sake. It wouldn't change anything, nor would it make the future any different.

"Oh, someone's been killed," Oliver said, as if he were merely mentioning the weather. "In a field, from what I can gather."

Langham told himself to accept the fact that neither of them were going to be able to get away from their calling in life. Oliver hearing that kind of thing then relating it to Langham was par for the course. Best to just accept it, get on with it as their lot. He digested the information. Had the fleeting but disturbing image of a woman sprawled out, much like one Oliver had found in the Sugar Strands case. Deaths in a field usually meant bodies being dumped, perhaps the result of supposedly missing persons who hadn't been missing at all but taken.

"Do we need to call anything in right this minute?" he asked, meaning that if the crimes had been committed ages ago, like those in the strawberry patch out the back of The Running Hare, there wasn't any urgency in the matter.

"Yep. It's recent. Less than an hour ago. And it isn't just some*one*—there's two of them."

"Jesus Christ. Let me know if we need to stop, if you get told where we need to go to find them."

"I know already. It's that big house up there." Oliver pointed ahead. "But we won't find anything. No bodies. Just a bit of blood in an office belonging to some old man called Colin."

"Two deaths in a field and possibly one inside then?" That made three—and definitely a good excuse not to get involved.

"Nope, just two. Colin was shot inside then killed outside."

What? "Oh, right. So the bodies have been disposed of?"

"You'll see."

Langham didn't press for more. If he were honest, he didn't want to know the ins and outs. He headed towards the house in the distance, frowning as a set of headlights outside it cut through the darkness about a mile away. Without having to ask, he knew the car belonged to the killers.

"Bloody hell," he said. "Get my phone out of my pocket, will you? Ring Fairbrother. He's going to be well and truly hacked off. He's got enough on his plate back in Marsh Vines."

Oliver reached across and fumbled for Langham's phone in his pocket. "The men who have been killed—I get the sense they deserved it, or at the very least that they were bad men themselves."

"Brilliant, just what we need. Probably a pair of burglars who got caught."

Oliver dialled Fairbrother's number. "It's more complex than that. And those men in that car... Well, one of them is bad, but at the same time I don't think he *likes* being bad. Not anymore anyway. I can see what he's thinking, clear as bloody day. He wants to start again, to pretend what he's done never happened. And he's done a lot."

"Many killers think that, Oliver. Feel remorse. Doesn't mean they should be allowed to get away with it, though."

"No, it doesn't."

The killers' car had come to the end of the driveway. The headlights spilled out onto the tarmac, cone-shaped slashes of brightness. While Oliver spoke to Fairbrother, Langham battled with feeling sick. Butterflies flapped about in his belly, and adrenaline had seeped out, on the verge of racing through him. The car ahead shot onto the main road, and Langham put his foot down.

"Fairbrother has sent someone out to intercept," Oliver said.

"Good. If backup get there first, we'll be able to go home. If not...possibly a long night ahead. And to be honest, we're so close it's bound to be us who pulls this one over."

Langham concentrated on the car, keeping a decent distance behind yet wanting to make sure he didn't lose sight of it. Mind you, out here in the middle of the night, he wasn't likely to—

"What the fuck?" he said.

Another vehicle had appeared at a T-junction at the end. A large black van. The car in front swerved and parked side-on, the screech of tyres setting Langham's teeth on edge. As Langham drew up to it then slowed to a stop, two men got out. One had long hair that flowed in the breeze, and the other was bald. The bald one turned, stared straight at Langham's car, the headlights illuminating him.

"Fucking Hiscock." Langham jabbed at his seat belt release button. "I knew he was up to something out here. I bloody—"

"Don't get out." Oliver flung his arm across to press his hand to Langham's belly. "If you get out, he'll shoot you."

"Shit. *Shit!*" Dread filled Langham, giving him that terrible weightless sensation he'd experienced so many times before, where he thought he'd either spew or shit himself.

"Let them go. He's got a gun in his waistband."

Langham toyed with getting out anyway, but Hiscock's face held a warning, one Langham didn't intend to ignore. He was going against his instinct—to apprehend.

"Fuck it!"

Hiscock and the long-haired man ran towards the van then got inside. It drove away, and Langham swore he caught sight of another familiar face.

"That sodding Sid Mondon!" He whacked the steering wheel with the heel of his hand. "Didn't I *say*, on the way here, that they were up to something?"

"You did."

"I knew. I bloody well *knew*."

"You did."

Langham took his phone from Oliver then rang Fairbrother. Their conversation was brief, with Langham relating what had happened, that their progress had been cut off by the car blocking the road and a van appearing to collect Hiscock and a man he'd never seen before.

"I didn't get a glimpse of the number plate of the van. We could go back to the house—mansion, more like," he said to Fairbrother, "but Oliver thinks there isn't any point. Whoever was killed there is long gone. So we'll stay here until someone else arrives—the car's parked across the turning, blocking us in, and I don't want anyone coming along and crashing into it."

"Right," Fairbrother said. "The thing is, as you know, I'm up to my armpits in it here. I've got Villier on her way out to you. She'll have to deal with it, because you need to get the hell home then fuck off on holiday. Like I said to you earlier, crime follows you, so all I can say is that wherever you're going, you'd better be prepared."

"Pack it in. I don't even want to think about it. Catch you soon."

Langham cut the call then got out of the car. He walked to the other one. The door was open from Hiscock's hasty exit, and the interior light showed nothing out of the ordinary inside. No blood.

Oliver joined him.

"I can't even begin to understand what's been going on at that house," Oliver said, "because from what this Colin is telling me, it's weird, like space-age stuff, and nothing is going to be found on the grounds."

"Shit. I'll let Villier know when she gets here, although what time that'll be is anyone's bloody guess."

He shoved his hands into his pockets and turned to look at the house. Lights were now on in the top floor windows—bright-orange lights.

"Oh, for Pete's sake!" Langham shouted. "That place is on fire!"

145

He called it in. By the time the fire crew appeared, the house may as well have been classed as gone. He clamped his eyes shut. He suspected something had been put on timer to make sure the place went up once Hiscock and that man were well away, otherwise it would have been on fire as the men had left. If he went over there now, there was no telling whether he'd be able to get inside—whether there was anyone in there who needed saving.

"Should I go there?" He opened his eyes and turned back to Oliver.

"No point. It's just dead bodies in there. The fire has to destroy something other than those. Colin says it's some sort of computer. It's very important that the fire is left to burn. At one time he'd have said the software should be saved, but he's been talking to Nellie, the woman from The Running Hare, and—"

"Jesus. He *knows* her?"

"Yeah. Since they were kids, apparently. Anyway, she's told him that the software is evil."

Langham laughed. "No more evil than she was, I'll bet."

Oliver shrugged. "Colin reckons she's changed. That he was surprised at what she'd done in life, but now she's gone back to how she was when he knew her. I'm trying not to get too involved in that side of it. Star-crossed lovers and all that. A love denied. Not my thing, is it."

"No. And waiting isn't my thing. I'm getting pissed off now."

The wait didn't turn out to be much longer. Villier arrived full of self-importance, as Langham had suspected she would. As a sergeant, she'd been trying hard to move up the ranks, but being a bolshie woman had seemed to prevent her career advancement. Maybe tonight she'd prove she could cope in what appeared to be a weird situation. Langham didn't want anything to do with it.

"Right," Villier said. "So you're saying we might need extra help out at the house?"

"Yes," Oliver said. "It's not your usual type of killing. I keep seeing a foreign country in my head, deserts and whatnot, and the feeling is strong that the kind of thing used to kill those people isn't something the general public know about. Covert weapons use, that sort of thing. Stuff governments keep quiet about. And one of the victims, a man named Colin, keeps saying his boss is someone in politics."

"Oh fuck." Villier chewed the inside of her cheek, stared behind them to where the mansion was. "So this investigation may well be taken off of us anyway then."

"I'd say so," Oliver said. "There are things going on that they won't want us knowing about."

"Yep, police involvement will be closed down," Langham said.

Villier grimaced. "I don't like that."

"Neither do I," Langham said, "but you'll come to realise that a lot of things are hushed up. Whether you like it or not, you need to do as you're told, keep your mouth shut, and just accept that the case isn't anything to concern yourself with once you're advised to step back. The fact that Hiscock and Mondon are involved, though... That's a surprise. They usually kill for hire, with guns. Still, if it means they'll be apprehended—finally—then that's a result in itself."

"Well." Villier gestured to an officer sitting in her patrol vehicle. "I need to get this car moved over, get it out of the way. And you two had best go. Suppose you'd be better off turning round and using an alternative route."

"Yep." And Langham was bloody glad to be doing that, too.

CHAPTER SEVENTEEN

"**W**hat the fucking hell are you two playing at?" Sid blasted down the road, gripping the steering wheel in his meaty hands. "First you ask me to sort it so a second man gets offed—which, by the way, is fine and dandy and done—but then you ask for a passport in a new name and want it at short notice. That isn't something I can manage within the hour, you know that. I mean, *really*?"

Jackson winced at the speed Sid was going. "If you don't slow down, we're going to get pulled over. I told you that bloody copper saw me. He'll have called it in—called the description of this van in."

"Yeah, yeah." Sid waved one hand. "Black vans are popular. Less popular than white, I'll give you that, but popular all the same. We could be anybody. Besides, it was the only one I had handy. All the others are out. And I'm well aware of that copper and what he'll have done—fucking stupid of you to have let him see you if you ask me—but I need to get us away from the scene pretty sharpish, don't I. Fuck me sideways, I know you're willing to pay handsomely, Mr Whiteling, and pardon my French, but some kind of warning would have been nice. I was about to go to bed."

"It's not his fault," Jackson said.

Jackson jabbed Sid in the ribs. Randall sat on Jackson's other side, and Jackson wondered now whether it had been a wise move for them to all sit in the front. Perhaps he and Randall should have climbed into the back. Sid, up front alone, would have aroused less suspicion. After all, he was just some overweight bloke, a man who never got a second glance. But Jackson, with his bald nut, and Randall with all that black hair? The police would spot them in no time and put two and two together.

"Stop the van," Jackson said.

"What?" Sid shook his head. "No bloody way. Not until we're out of range and where we need to be. And pulling over now isn't a good idea, look."

Blue lights swirled ahead. Jackson's guts rolled. The lights belonged to a fire engine, going by the height of them. That was the second one he'd seen. Shit, would the computer be sufficiently burnt already? Jackson stared at Randall.

"I have the hard drive," Randall said.

"I see."

"I'll destroy it elsewhere."

The fire engine barrelled past, the speed of it rocking the van. The sudden blare of its siren, unnecessary given that they were in the countryside in the middle of the night, had Jackson unnerved. He didn't like feeling so out of sorts, so on the verge of being caught. Never had he experienced this in all his time of working for Sid.

Sid turned onto a narrow track, and they continued their journey at a slower speed. Feeling it was less likely they were going to be pulled over, Jackson relaxed, allowing his body to sink into the seat.

"Listen," Sid said, "and listen good. There's a place you can stay while the passport is being sorted. I also need you, Mr Whiteling, to allow me online access to your bank so I can get you a new account, one that no one will find, if you catch my drift. Debit cards also need to be made that match the new account and the name you'll be going by after tonight. This is a complete break, understand? No going back. No contacting anyone. It wouldn't be so bad if I knew this wasn't going to come back on me in some way, but it might. I'm going to be questioned as to why I was probably spotted picking you up on a country road in the middle of nowhere." He cleared his throat. "Of course, the money Mr Whiteling will be paying can buy many things, including an alibi from the usual tart who covers my arse from time to time, but that's not the point. Never been caught for anything in my life, but this might be the one time where I get hauled behind bars. It's not on."

"But it's what you do," Jackson said. "The only difference between Mr Whiteling and another client is that he asked you to come and get us. Why didn't you send Gail? She would have done it."

"She was busy on another job—they all are. I was the only one left."

"And greed is why you said yes to helping us out," Jackson said. "Don't make out you're doing this begrudgingly or that we forced you. Money is always your motive, and even if you thought what you were doing would be dangerous, you'd do it anyway if it meant upping your bank balance."

Sid laughed. "Fucking hell, am I sitting on Dr Phil's sofa or what?"

Jackson didn't bother speaking further. He'd said his piece, and that was the end of it.

What appeared to be a farmhouse without any lights on came into view. Set off the road, it was surrounded by trees, ensuring the property was well hidden. Sid turned off the track and onto a driveway, gaining speed as if the desire to get to the place had overtaken him. Once outside the property, Sid parked then cut the engine. He got out. Walked to the front door. Knocked. Waited.

"What the hell's he doing?" Randall asked.

"This must be the place he mentioned."

Sid disappeared inside the house, swallowed by the darkness. He reappeared and beckoned for them to join him. They got out of the van. Inside the cottage with the door closed, Jackson wandered blindly down a dark hallway until they reached a door. Sid opened it, and light spilled out, showcasing a splash of red wall with white wainscoting. They filed inside; the windows had blackout material covering them. A man stood in front of one, a white backdrop on a stand beside him, a chair in front of that. Jackson studied him— in his forties, greying at the temples, a moustache that belonged in nineteen twenty-five. He wasn't a threat.

"You'll need to cut your hair off," the man said, nodding at Randall. "Still, small price to pay for a bit of freedom, eh? Come on then, take a pew."

Randall did as he was told.

"That'll do nicely." The bloke collected a camera on a tripod from the corner and put it in front of Randall. "Keep still. And don't scowl. That hair..." He grabbed a cordless set of clippers. "Like I said, it needs to come off."

The buzzing of the clippers went on for ages then stopped. Randall appeared so different. Jackson wouldn't have known it was him if it wasn't for those piercing eyes.

Photos were taken of Randall, then the photographer walked over to a computer in the corner. He plugged the camera into it. "You may as well go and get some sleep. Rooms are upstairs. The passport won't be ready for a while yet. Got any name preference?"

Randall shook his head. "No. Best you choose it."

"Fine," he said. "On you go then."

Jackson stared at Sid, silently asking if it was okay that they stayed here. This hadn't been fully discussed, and he wasn't sure if he was completely happy with it.

"Dick's all right, aren't you, Dick?" Sid said. "Always has the windows blacked out so it seems like the place is abandoned. Got a brilliant alarm system, and, would you bloody believe it, there's an underground getaway wotsit. You know, one of them tunnel things."

Jackson felt a little better.

"I need those bank details," Sid said to Randall. "And don't worry, I won't fiddle you out of any money that I'm not due."

Randall fished his wallet from his pocket then handed over his bank card, giving him a code to log in online.

"That's the ticket," Sid said. "I'll pick you up in the morning or whenever the passport is ready and your flight has been booked."

Upstairs, Jackson chose a room at the front so he could nose outside if any vehicles came— providing he peeled back the blackout material that was attached by Velcro. Jackson looked around. Simple IKEA-like furnishings. Most definitely a guest room used by people just like him.

He sat on the end of the bed.

Everything would turn out all right, wouldn't it? *If we don't get caught.*

"Fuck it. I'm sodding off an' all." He legged it back downstairs and approached the bloke. "I need a passport."

The fella laughed. "Fuck me. Hang on. Let me just find a wig to cover your bonce."

CHAPTER EIGHTEEN

Abroad at last. Who'd have thought it, eh?
Bleary-eyed, Langham stared at himself in the bathroom mirror. It was different from the one back home. For one, it was lightly speckled with rust spots, and two, the light was so severe it seemed to bounce off the white tiles, into the mirror then back out at him. It wouldn't be so bad

if he had a hangover so he could blame the pain in his eyes from the brightness on that. But since it was just because he was tired, as usual… He'd remedy that by napping on the beach in an hour or so.

Spain was just what they needed. Turquoise ocean, white sands.

This morning was the start of their holiday at last—*thank bloody God*—but Langham had been unable to sleep properly last night. Although he'd sunk a few beers in an attempt to help him sleep, as usual he'd let his hunches interfere with his well-being. On the plane, he could have sworn he'd seen a man who resembled Jackson Hiscock, except it couldn't have been. That bloke had hair, a beard, and the man he'd been with had a military cut, not a long style. Langham had caught their attention on purpose by walking past and nudging the armrest with his knee on the way to the toilet, but not one ounce of recognition had flickered on their faces. He'd told himself he'd been wrong but…

I'm not convinced.

He left the bathroom, slightly more awake now he'd brushed his teeth, and joined Oliver in the kitchen area of the open-plan space. This apartment was deceptive. From the outside it looked small, yet once inside it was spacious. He could imagine living abroad permanently, although when it came down to it, he doubted he'd be able to leave the city of his birth and give up his job.

Oliver had prepared fruit from the complimentary bowl that had awaited them when they'd arrived. Mango, pineapple, and guava by the look of it. Langham took a seat on a red plastic stool at the breakfast bar, and Oliver joined him, placing cups of hot green tea on the worktop then handing Langham a fork.

"I can't believe we're here," Oliver said. "It's another world. Like the city and our life there doesn't exist. It isn't until you get away that you see the difference. Feel the difference. And the spirits, Christ, they're so polite."

The spirits. Would they ever leave Oliver alone? Langham doubted it, and Oliver wouldn't be Oliver if he didn't carry them around with him twenty-four-seven. Caring about them, trying to help them fully pass over.

"How do you mean, polite?" Langham popped a square of guava in his mouth.

"Well, they're not pushy," Oliver said. "And when I tell them I'm on holiday, they back off."

"Thank fuck for that." Langham laughed. "We might well get a bit of peace after all."

"We will if you stop thinking about Jackson Hiscock and that man."

Langham closed his eyes briefly. Was it that obvious? Was he that transparent? "Christ, sorry."

"It's fine. Listen, if I tell you something, will you promise not to go off on one?"

"Go off on one? I wouldn't do that to you, man." At least he didn't think he would.

"I know. Figure of speech. I know how you've pledged to uphold the law and whatever, but if

159

there was something I knew and I didn't say, and you found out I didn't say, you'd be narked, wouldn't you?"

"Probably."

"And I wasn't going to say anything but I feel I should."

Langham's gut contracted. This didn't sound good at all. "Depends what it is."

"It's something to do with knowing something," Oliver said. "And if I don't tell you, tell the police, then I'm just as bad as a criminal, but..." He gnawed lightly at his bottom lip. Stared out of the window for a few seconds, then turned his head so he looked at Langham again. "Okay. Right. That *was* Hiscock on the plane. There. I've said it. Done. Now you can do what you will with the information."

Langham took in a deep breath then pushed it out through pursed lips. "I *knew* it. Those bloody eyes of his..." But what did he want to do about it? "What did they do? In the mansion, I mean."

"Hiscock shot Colin in self-defence—Colin had drawn a gun on him first—but he didn't kill him. Neither did the man he was with. A machine killed Colin. Software, whatever. But Hiscock is here in disguise." Oliver chuckled. "And I'd guess it killed Hiscock wearing a wig in this heat when we landed."

"I'll bet it fucking did. I have to call it in, you know—I'll text Fairbrother and let him deal with it. But if I see him here, where we are, if they didn't go off to another resort, then I'll tell the police here. I don't care if he didn't kill that Colin bloke,

160

he has killed others. I just haven't been able to prove it or had sufficient grounds to arrest him, question him."

"They're not here," Oliver said. "When we landed, they got a bus elsewhere."

"Well, then. That solves it. Time to enjoy this holiday." Langham sighed.

Crime could just go and do one. He'd had enough of it.

For now.

Printed in Great Britain
by Amazon